NATHAN COLLINS

The Last Monument

For more about Nathan, visit www.nates.pics

First edition

ISBN: 979-8-89686-390-8

This book was professionally typeset on Reedsy.
Find out more at reedsy.com

Contents

Foreword

The world we know is shrinking. We are all being squeezed into a box, a carefully constructed reality where the lines between order and oppression blur. Creativity, that unpredictable force that has propelled humanity for years, is now viewed with suspicion, a dangerous deviation from the set path.

This story is a whisper in the wind, a testament to the enduring power of the human spirit to create, to imagine, to dream. It is a testament to the architects of our dreams, those who dare to challenge the boundaries, to build beyond the confines of the known.

This is a story for those who feel the stifling grip of societal control, for those who yearn for a world where imagination is not a threat, but a celebration. It is a story about the last architect, who, faced with the daunting task of encapsulating the essence of humanity in a single structure, finds himself grappling with the very essence of his being.

Let it serve as a reminder that even in the face of seemingly impossible obstacles, the human spirit can soar. Let it inspire you to break free from the confines of your own reality and embrace the boundless possibilities of your imagination.

Acknowledgments

This book began as a modest idea for a short film I wanted to create. I took a lot of inspiration from several different sources, including my internship at a structural engineering firm. Past books fueled my ideas, my day-to-day drives gave me new words to describe the monotony in Malcolm's hometown. Hell, even music was a major source of emotion and feeling for this book. This story may be fiction, but its foundation is deeply rooted in the world we live in. The world of *The Last Monument* is not our world today, but it is one that feels just close enough to touch, with the rise of artificial intelligence, the creation of rigid and unrelenting political systems, and all of the silent compromises people make in their day-to-day lives.

I've written short stories since second grade and had these big dreams of becoming a famous celebrity known for my creativity and imagination, similar to every other second-grader.

I think that Malcolm takes a lot after his creator in this biographical dystopian fiction. I tried my best to write about things that I could relate to so that I could express the raw feelings of it all to the readers—from the use of Adderall to the struggles of finding peace internally and always feeling as though I can better myself. This book is a piece of fiction, but in a way, I think it could serve as guidance for many people who face internal struggles on a day-to-day basis.

I would like to acknowledge all the people who supported

me through this journey of creation. I'd also like to thank all the people who pre-ordered this book as well, and I'd like to thank the people who questioned me when I told them about this book—your skepticism fueled my determination, and for that, I am truly grateful.

WARNING

vii

THIS BOOK HAS BEEN RESTRICTED PER THE *CONTENT STANDARDIZATION ACT*

November

I stare at the blank canvas before me, a vast white expanse mocking my inability to fill it. The weight of my first commission pressed down on me—a physical burden that squeezed the air from my lungs. I graduated summa cum laude from Cooper Union on a Tuesday, I landed an entry-level position at Meridian Associates by Thursday, and I got my first commission on the Monday after that. The firm specializes in commercial real estate – the kind of soulless, cost-effective structures that fill the spaces between places people actually want to be. Everybody has to start somewhere, though. My desk was in the corner of the rented high-rise office, wedged between a filing cabinet and a dying ficus tree. The plant would cast shadows that looked like fractal patterns. I must have spent more time studying those than my actual work.

My first commission was for a strip mall in Newark. A functional structure with an attached parking garage. A standard glass and steel box. No hidden mathematics or design. It's funny because I chose this profession years ago, drawn to its power to shape landscapes, to create spaces that resonated with human emotion—yet, here I sit designing a parking garage for a strip mall that nobody will shop at. The client was Mr. Hammond. He wore a sleek Armani suit that cost more than my monthly salary and carried a gold-plated fountain pen he never actually used. The ink surely dried up months ago. He had approached our firm with a simple request: maximize profit per square foot. That's all architecture really is now – the art of turning space into money. He came carrying a tablet loaded with the New Architecture Guidelines. Every developer carried them now, ever since the Efficiency in Design Act passed last spring. The Guidelines were clear: no decorative elements without practical purpose, no abstract forms, no "unnecessarily complex" geometric patterns. Architecture had been reduced to a simple equation: maximum utility divided by minimum cost.

The design brief Hammond hands me comes in a gray folder stamped with the Department of Architectural Standardization's seal. Inside, every parameter is precisely defined. Maximum height. Minimum parking spaces. Approved materials. Acceptable angles. The only decision left to make is which pre-approved design template to modify. I stare at the blank drafting schemes in front of me. My eyes glance back and forth from the gray folder to the empty screen, as if I'm waiting for the design to assemble itself before me. My eyes move down to my desk drawer. I open it and stare at the bottle of small pills, innocent as the blank drafting pages spread across my screen. 10mg of focus. Of necessity. Of surrender. The Adderall feels heavier than it should, like it's dense with all the thoughts it will force into coherence. I take one without water to wash it down my dry throat.

The Adderall kicks in as I review the approved templates. The world narrows to clean lines and right angles, all the messy possibilities condensed into acceptable outcomes. Template A-117 seems the most promising – it meets all efficiency metrics while maintaining the illusion of design choice. I begin the modifications, each click of my mouse a compromise between what could be and what's allowed to be.

"Good choice," David says during the afternoon review. "A-117 has the highest client satisfaction rating in the tri-state area." He scrolls through my modifications, nodding at each minor adjustment. "Though…" he pauses at my window arrangement, frowning slightly. "These spacing variations. They're within tolerance, but they seem… intentional."

They are intentional.

Even through the haze of the Adderall, I couldn't help trying to add in a pattern, a sequence, anything that resembled something other than a concrete block. They decided patterns were too unpredictable. "I'll standardize them," I promise, already reaching for another pill. The second pill dissolves on my tongue as David leaves, bitter and chalky like the taste of compromise. The office grows quieter as the afternoon stretches on, the gentle hum of computers and shuffling papers creating a monotonous symphony. Through my window, I can see the city skyline – a testament to what architecture used to be. The old buildings stand like aging giants among the newer, standardized structures. Their spires and ornate facades seem to mock us.

I pull up the window specifications again, my fingers hovering over the keyboard. The Fibonacci sequence had always fascinated me – nature's perfect pattern, appearing in everything from seashells to galaxies. The window spacing I'd designed followed it subtly, each distance a careful calculation that would appear random to the untrained eye. But David had noticed. Of course he had. He'd been in the industry long enough to remember when architects were still allowed to create.

My phone suddenly buzzes to life. Claire. She sent one word: "Lunch?"

Claire works in the Archive Department two floors down. We met during orientation – she was the only other person who seemed to be suffocating under the weight of all the gray paint and mass-produced IKEA minimalism—white desks, ergonomic chairs, and generic wall art designed to please no one and offend no one in the firm. She used to be an art student. Now she catalogs old architectural drawings, preparing them for eventual disposal. "Preserving history," they call it, though we both know it's more about erasing it.

"Can't. Deadline." I text back, though my stomach seems to not like that answer. The Adderall doesn't help. I force myself to focus on the standardization. Window spacing: 1.5 meters. Material: approved energy-efficient glass. Tint: 35% exactly. No variation. No pattern. No life. The afternoon blurs into the evening as I meticulously erase every trace of creativity from the design. Each deletion feels like I'm chipping away at something inside myself.

I finally finish, but I don't feel accomplished. I submit "Template A-117, Modified Version 2.4" with all parameters within acceptable ranges. The confirmation email arrives instantly: "Design Submission Accepted. Efficiency Rating: 94.2%. Cost-Effectiveness Rating: 96.1%. Standardization Compliance: 100%." I should feel proud. These are good numbers for a first commission. Instead, I find myself opening my desk drawer again, staring at the pill bottle. Three taken today. A new record. The old buildings outside my window have disappeared into the darkness, leaving only the uniform glow of the new structures – perfect boxes of light arranged in perfect rows.

My phone buzzes again. Claire: "Roof? I brought dinner." I hesitate, then grab my jacket. The roof of our building is technically off-limits after hours, but Claire discovered that the security system doesn't monitor the service entrance. Is it illegal? No. Is it frowned upon? Don't care. Am I doing it anyway? Obviously.

It sounds cliche, but it's actually one of the few places left in the city where you can still see stars between the buildings. The night air sobers me up as I push open the heavy metal door. Claire sits cross-legged near the edge, a small paper bag beside her. Her dark hair whips around her face in the wind, and for a moment, she looks like she could be in one of those old modeling magazines from before.

"You look terrible," she says, patting the concrete beside her. "How many today?"

I sit down, avoiding her eyes. "Three."

She doesn't say anything, instead, she pulls a sandwich from her bag, tears it in half, and hands me a piece. "You know what they used to call architects?" she asks, taking a bite. "Master builders. Artists of space and light. Now look at us – you're a template modifier, and I'm a professional eraser." "At least we're efficient about it," I say, chuckling. We eat in silence, watching the city below. From up there all the lights blur together, creating patterns that would never be approved by the Department of Architectural Standardization. I laugh to myself. A gentle rain begins to fall, and I watch as the droplets create chaotic patterns on the roof's surface – another form of disorder that would need to be controlled if they could figure out how.

"I found something today in the archives," Claire says finally, her voice barely above a whisper. "A design from before. It was beautiful, Malcolm. Curves and angles that made no sense but somehow made perfect sense. It looked like it was growing out of the earth itself." She pauses, wiping rain from her face. "I had to mark it for deletion." I think about my window spacing, my subtle attempt at rebellion through mathematics. "Sometimes I wonder if we're the last ones," I say. "The last generation to remember what it was like when buildings could be beautiful."

"We're not the last ones," Claire replies, but her voice lacks conviction. "I think we're just the ones who have to watch it end."

"I made a copy," she says, pressing it into my hand. "Before I had to delete it. Don't let anyone see it." Claire looks at me for a moment, almost lovingly. She gets up and says bye, closing the heavy metal door behind her.

Back in my apartment, I unfold the paper carefully. It's a hand-drawn sketch of a building that would never be approved today. The structure seems to defy gravity, with sweeping arches and intricate details that serve no purpose except to be beautiful. In the corner, barely legible, is a date. It was years ago, but it feels like another century. I pin the sketch to the wall behind my desk, covering it with a calendar. Tomorrow, I'll go back to another Template A-117. I'll standardize more windows and calculate additional efficiency ratings. I'll take my pills and meet my deadlines. But tonight, I let myself remember why I wanted to be an architect. I fall asleep at my desk, the forbidden sketch hidden behind my calendar, and dream of buildings that dance.

When I wake, my neck is stiff and my mouth is dry. A side effect of the Adderall. The rain has stopped, leaving streaks on the window. The city glows in the pre-dawn light, a mix of old grace and new efficiency that makes my heart ache. My phone shows 4:47 AM – too early to head to the office, too late to try for real sleep. Instead, I flick the television on and watch last night's news. It's another clip of statues being torn down. I think about how we got here—how everything got so sanitized. How architecture lost its soul.

They called it the Denver Incident. I was still in undergrad school then, more interested in applied mathematics than politics. A recently constructed, massive, abstract sculpture, meant to represent community resilience, became the flashpoint of the news. Its flowing, ambiguous forms sparked different interpretations from various political groups. What started as peaceful demonstrations escalated into weeks of civil unrest. I pull up an old photo on my phone – the sculpture stands twisted and bold against the Rocky Mountains, its metal surface catching the sunlight in ways that would never pass today's Guidelines. I remember watching Senator Walsh's speech with my parents during Christmas break when they were still together, her words echoing through our living room: "Art, in its most provocative forms, serves as a catalyst for social upheaval." My father, an old-school architect who'd retired rather than adapt, had thrown his coffee mug at the TV. My mother had quietly taken down the abstract paintings from our walls the next day. "Just until things settle down," she'd said. They never went back up. Dad never replaced his mug.

The Architectural Stability Act was passed during my sophomore year at Cooper Union. Professor Chen had devoted an entire class to discussing it, though he was careful with his words. "The Department of Architectural Standardization will ensure safety and efficiency," he'd said, his face carefully neutral. But after class, I'd found him in his office, shredding his collection of design magazines. Changes came gradually after that. First, they modified our curriculum. "Practical Architecture for Modern Needs" replaced "Design Theory and Innovation." Our software gained new "compliance checkers" that flagged anything too original. By my junior year, half our professors had retired or "transitioned to administrative roles."

I pull out my desk drawer and count my remaining Adderall. Twenty-three pills. Almost enough to finish the month, if I'm careful. They started prescribing it to architecture students during my senior year – "focus enhancement for optimal standardization compliance." Most of us were already taking it anyway, struggling to suppress our creative impulses and focus on approved templates. The morning light grows stronger, catching the edge of my hidden sketch. I think about my father's last building before he retired – a small library on the outskirts of town. They're scheduled to "renovate" it next year, to bring it up to current standards. To erase its soul, like they're erasing everything else.

The Barrett Institute study came out just before graduation. "Exposure to non-traditional architectural designs correlates with increased rates of questioning authority and non-conventional thinking among young people." The study was flawed – Claire showed me the methodology holes – but it didn't matter. By then, people wanted to believe that standardization would keep us safe. Keep us "in our right minds." It was a step towards diminishing the youth. Removing the people who didn't "fit in" our society would surely be next— but for now, the structures we surround ourselves with would take the hit.

My phone shows an alert: Version 6.0 of the ArchiSync Compliance Guidelines drops next week. I scroll through the preview: "Enhanced window spacing regulations... Prohibition of intentional pattern recognition triggers… Updated compliance scoring algorithms…" Each revision feels like another brick in a wall between us and creativity. I think about the buildings that inspired me to become an architect. The Guggenheim's spiral. Gaudí's organic forms. The dancing curves of Zaha Hadid. All of them would be illegal now, classified as "unnecessarily complex" and "psychologically disruptive." They let us study them in school, but only as historical artifacts, like examining extinct species. Claire says we're not the last ones to remember beauty, but sometimes I wonder. The junior architects at our firm, fresh out of school, don't even seem to notice what's missing. They talk about efficiency ratings and compliance scores with genuine enthusiasm. Last week, one of them reported a senior architect for using the golden ratio in his design plans. "Unnecessary pattern implementation," the report said. He was suspended for three weeks.

The sun rises fully now, painting the city in shades of pink and gold. For a moment, the light transforms the standardized buildings, creating illusions of depth and texture that would never pass inspection. I think about the Denver sculpture, about how it meant something different to everyone who saw it. That was its power, they said. That was why it had to go. That was why everything had to change. People just wanted to feel appreciated, seen. The Denver project did just that: made everyone feel like someone. The government didn't appreciate how something could unite whole cities. When it was removed, sure there was an uproar. For 2 weeks maximum. After that, people just blended back into the crowds. Yet, the possibility of it happening again was too much of a risk—a liability—for the government. Slow implementations of ordinances, acts, laws, and eventually amendments. All to make sure that everybody knew their place. Constitutionally correct? Sure. Morally? Ethically? Anything else-ly? Not at all.

My father used to say that architecture was frozen music. Now it's just frozen, rigid, safe. The new buildings don't inspire riots or revolution. They don't inspire anything at all. Maybe that's the point.

Before work, I like to wander through the park, enjoying a break from the straight lines and rigid angles I draw every day. It's funny – the trees grow wherever the hell they want, twisting and arching, and somehow nobody slaps a guideline on them. At least not yet. I pause by the pond, watching ripples dance across the surface in patterns no software could ever predict. A duck gives me a hard look, like it's judging my whole life, and lets out a loud quack before leaving a gift right next to my shoe. I mutter a "Thanks" and keep walking. I sit down on a blocky, concrete, bench made to deter homeless people from sleeping on it. I cautiously take out my sketchbook – actual paper – and quickly draw the scene before me: the trees caught in the morning light, the old buildings beyond the park standing proud among the new ones, and the way the shadows of the leaves create unexpected patterns. It reminds me of the ficus tree in my office. I should take care of it more.

In an hour, I'll have to go to work. I'll take my pills, open Template A-117, and continue turning spaces into money. But for now, I let myself remember what it was like to dream in three dimensions. My daydream is cut short as my phone buzzes. A message from Claire: "They're moving up the library renovation. Your dad's building. Next month." I look at the sketch I just made before sliding it into my bag. Maybe I'll show it to my father when I visit him this weekend. He lives in a standardized assisted-living apartment complex now, all right angles and approved colors. But he still draws sometimes, on napkins and in the margins of *New York Times* sudoku, or *The Gazette*'s daily crossword when he thinks no one is watching.

Another buzz: David, my boss. "Client meeting at 11. Bring the final renders." I tuck the sketchbook away and reach for my pill bottle. One last look at the morning sky. I find myself cloud-watching a lot now, there is more life in the lifeless clouds than there is around me sometimes. My office is only a couple minutes worth of walking from the park—I make sure to take my time. Template A-117 waits for me, its clean lines and standardized spaces. I take a pill and empty my backpack to get ready for work. I take out my water bottle and make sure to give my green office companion a good drink.

December

December brought with it a particular kind of cold that seemed to seep through the window seals. Though, to be fair, they worked better than the "artistic" windows in my childhood home, which leaked like they were designed by someone who thought drafts were avant-garde. The city is stained gray with the overcast clouds. The ficus tree beside my desk had dropped another leaf – I'd been counting. Thirty-seven since I started at Meridian. Each one a tiny funeral for something natural and unpredictable.

I water the dying ficus tree beside my new desk – I insisted on bringing it from my old corner when they promoted me after Mr. Hammond's project. I guess they really liked it. David raised an eyebrow but didn't object; plants are still considered "productivity-enhancing natural elements" according to Section 7.3 of the Guidelines. The tree continues its slow decline though, dropping leaves that cast ever-shifting shadows on my drafting table. Sometimes I think it's dying out of protest, refusing to thrive in this sterile environment. But even its decay creates beauty – the remaining leaves cast the all familiar fractal patterns that remind me of the intricate details we're no longer allowed to design.

"You know what's funny?" Claire says, walking into my

office. "You could have knocked." I mutter. I scramble to hide the doodles that I was drawing—more unauthorized patterns. She perches on my desk with a turkey sandwich dangling precariously over my keyboard. "Those old Brutalist buildings from the '60s? They're basically what we're designing now, except ours will actually outlast the heat death of the universe." She takes a bite and crumbs scatter across my carefully organized desktop.

"Watch the keyboard," I mutter, brushing away sandwich debris. "And yeah, that's because everything's precast concrete and synthetic wood now. No maintenance issues when there's nothing interesting enough to break."

"Reminds me of you sometimes, Mal." Claire says sarcastically. "You've really been on edge since your dad's library renovation project started." She was right.

"You know, you're the only person I know who'd fight to keep a dying tree," Claire says, still perching on the edge of my desk. She pokes at a yellowing leaf. "Though I have to admit, it's probably the most interesting thing in this whole building. Even its death is more creative than Template A-117."

"Hey, A-117 got me this corner office," I protest, but I'm smiling. "Besides, the tree's not dying. It's expressing individualistic tendencies through organic decomposition."

"Sounds like someone's been reading too many compliance reports. You sound like David." I find myself laughing for the first time in days. Claire has that effect – finding humor in our dull lives. She continues to eat her sandwich, except she leans over the trash can this time.

My desk drawer holds four bottles of Adderall now. The doctor doubled my prescription after reviewing my productivity metrics. "Your compliance scores show remarkable consistency," she'd said, not looking up from her tablet. "We want to maintain that." I don't tell her that I'm taking them to dull the pain of watching my father's library being "upgraded" this week. I read the notice sitting on my desk again. This may be the 20th time I've done so. The renovation notice arrived last Tuesday, printed on the usual standardized gray paper with the Department's seal:

NOTICE OF MANDATORY ARCHITECTURAL COMPLIANCE UPGRADE
  Re: Robertson Memorial Library, 1247 Maple Street
  Current Efficiency Rating: 62.3%
  Target Efficiency Rating: 95%+
  Renovation Schedule: December 15-23

"You can't just measure a building's worth in efficiency ratings," Claire says, reading the notice with me. "Some things can't be quantified." She's been coming up to my office more often lately, usually with coffee, her sandwich, and conversation that makes me feel less numb.

My father hasn't left his apartment since I showed him the notice. He designed that library years ago, his last project before retirement. It was – and still is – beautiful in ways that are hard to explain now. The reading rooms follow the sun throughout the day. Light moves through the space like music. The shelves curve gently, creating quiet nooks that feel like secrets. Children loved to play hide-and-seek there. All of that will be gone by Christmas.

I think about the library's main hall, how the afternoon light catches dust in the air and turns them into dancing constellations. "They'll standardize the windows first," I tell her.

"Replace the hand-carved woodwork with approved synthetic materials. Straighten all the curves." My voice catches.

"Let's go see it," Claire says suddenly. "The library. Before they start tomorrow. I want to see what real architecture looks like one last time. And it would be good for you, I think." I don't protest, or go back to work after my lunch break, either.

The sun is setting by the time we arrive, casting long shadows through the library's western windows. The cleaning crew knows me – I've been coming here since I was a kid – and they let us in after hours. Claire walks slowly through the main hall, running her hand along the curved shelves, looking up at the way the ceiling seems to float above us. I show her my father's hidden touches: the subtle Fibonacci spiral in the floor pattern, the golden ratio in the shelf heights, the way certain angles align perfectly during the solstices. "He built it to grow old beautifully," I tell her. "The wood was supposed to darken over time, the brass handles were meant to develop a patina from thousands of hands touching them." We end up sitting on the floor in the children's section, surrounded by books that somehow escaped the Content Standardization Act. Claire leans against a shelf, her hair catching the last rays of sunlight. "Tell me about when he designed it," she says. "What was it like when architects could still create?" I tell her about sitting in my father's home office, watching him sketch iteration after iteration. How he'd wake up at 3 AM with new ideas, how he'd spend hours getting the curve of a single wall just right. "He used to say that every building should have at least one detail that makes people stop and wonder," I say. "Something that rewards attention."

"Like what?" Claire asks, moving closer. I take her hand and lead her to the central skylight. "Wait for it," I whisper. As the sun hits the horizon, light catches the glass skylights and refracts in a way that can't be described. For just a few minutes, the entire ceiling dances with rainbow patterns. Claire's face lights up with wonder, and suddenly I'm seeing the library through new eyes – not just as something I'm about to lose, but as something I was lucky to have known at all.

The next morning, the renovation crews arrives. I watch from across the street as they set up their equipment. Claire stands beside me, her shoulder touching mine, as the first window comes out. By noon, half the western face has been stripped of my father's carefully chosen woodwork. The crews work with mechanical efficiency – they've done this hundreds of times before. That evening, I bring my father to see it. It took a lot of convincing. He stands in silence, leaning heavily on his cane, as workers install the new regulation-compliant windows. They're perfectly rectangular, evenly spaced, utterly predictable. No more rainbow refractions, no more dancing light. I can't bear to watch the defacing anymore.

I leave for home. I have work the next day.

I arrive on time the next morning, before I can even sit down at my desk, David appears at my office entrance. "Malcolm, good news. The developer in Newark, what's-his-face, loved your modifications to A-117. Said he would be, quote, 'putting in a good word' for you."

"Thanks, David. I really tried to make it as forgettable as possible."

"That's the spirit!" David either misses or ignores the sarcasm. He beams like this is the highest praise imaginable. Maybe now it is. I glance at my phone – a text from Dad. He's sent a few since the renovation started. This one is just a photo: workers removing the last of the curved glass panels from the library's reading room. The ones he'd designed to cast shadow patterns that changed with the seasons. "Progress," I text back, because what else can I say? The ficus drops another leaf. Thirty-nine.

Lately, I've been having treasonous thoughts about standardization. Not that I'd admit it to Claire, but some of it makes sense. The new buildings are incredibly energy efficient. They're cheaper to maintain. They last longer. No more planned obsolescence like in the early 2010s, when developers deliberately used materials that would need replacing in twenty years. I think about the medical centers and hospitals that follow the new structural codes. About how they will probably still be standing in a hundred years, its standardized corridors guiding patients through standardized procedures. Maybe that's not always a bad thing for a hospital. Some buildings don't need to be beautiful. Some buildings just need to function. Maybe it's better like that.

The renovation takes five days. I avoid visiting, but I can't avoid the progress reports that pop up on my tablet. And I can't avoid Dad's messages, either. Each update reads like a clinical diagnosis:

Day 1: Removal of unnecessary architectural elements complete
Day 2: Installation of approved materials 47% complete
Day 3: Installation of approved materials 76% complete
Day 4: Installation of approved materials 91% complete
Day 5: Final standardization and efficiency optimization in progress

On the morning of the sixth day, I get another text from Dad. No photo this time, just words: "It's done." The library renovation is complete. Two days ahead of schedule, thanks to standardized construction methods. I take the afternoon off and drive out to see it. Claire comes with me, her hand finding mine as we stand in the parking lot, staring at what used to be my father's last creative statement. The curves are gone, replaced by clean lines and right angles. The windows are perfectly spaced, no more seasonal shadow plays. It looks… efficient. "I'm sorry," Claire whispers.

"The funny thing is," I say, "it'll probably last longer now. Dad's design… the curved glass was already showing wear. The unique fixtures were getting harder to replace. This version… this one could stand for centuries."

"And no one will ever look at it twice… I wanted to show you something." Claire says. She leads me inside, the warm woods have been replaced with cool grays and whites. The curves are gone, every angle calculated for maximum efficiency. The windows are perfectly standardized, the specialty ones removed and recycled. It looks like most other buildings now – clean, safe, soulless. But that's not what Claire wanted to show me. She leads me to the children's section, where my father had hidden so many small design treasures. The renovation crews have stripped away the old shelving, revealing something on the back wall. There, carved into the concrete foundation itself, is a spiral pattern. My father's signature, literally built into the bones of the building.

"They can't remove it without compromising the structure," Claire says, running her fingers over the pattern. "It's part of the foundation now."

I stare at the spiral, thinking about patterns that persist, about trees that refuse to grow straight, about small acts of rebellion hidden in concrete and shadow. Some things are made to resist.

We stand there for a long while, looking, waiting, watching people enter and exit the building without once looking around.

No one seems to notice that anything has changed. Maybe that's the real victory of standardization – it's made us stop looking.

On the seventh day since the renovation began, I arrive at work to find my ficus tree has dropped more leaves. They lay scattered around my desk like abandoned dreams. I find one of the ficus tree's leaves on my keyboard. The pattern of its veins reminds me of the library's old floor plan. I tape it to my monitor, next to my compliance metrics. Claire brings Starbucks and sits with me while I sweep up the fragile leaves off my once spotless office floor.

On my screen, my new commission—Template B-224—waits for my input, its clean lines and predictable angles ready to become another forgettable building. The new project will be perfectly compliant, perfectly efficient, perfectly unmemorable. But somewhere, in the spacing of the windows or the angle of the entrance, there might be something only Claire would notice. Something almost like creativity. "The tree's not dead, you know," Claire says to me. "It's just waiting for spring." I look at her, this woman who brings me coffee and hope that's too real, and I think maybe she's right. Maybe we're all just waiting for spring, for the moment when the patterns we've hidden in concrete and shadow finally bloom again.

The ficus drops another leaf. Fifty-seven.

As Christmas approaches, the city's muted celebrations filter in through the office's frosted windows. Snow falls in tidy intervals, like someone programmed the weather to match the holiday. A generic wreath hangs in the lobby, its artificial greenery just as uniform as the rest of the building. December's usual grayness is softened by a hint of festive lights on the city's main streets. The decorations are modest this year, nothing like the elaborate, tangled displays of my childhood, but they're there – a glow at every street corner and a quiet melody piped into public spaces. The Christmas trees, perfectly pruned and identical in height, line the plaza outside my office. They're uniform, yes, but Claire tells me she saw a child try to place a homemade ornament on one earlier, and it stayed there all afternoon.

Holiday decorations, like everything else, adhere to regulatory guidelines: safe, minimal, in neutral colors with a standardized ratio of green to red. Yet the occasional glint of tinsel in the wrong place, a patch of frost on an undecorated window, or the whisper of a real, unscheduled carol gives the city a flicker of unregulated warmth. It's as though the holiday manages to slip through the cracks in regulation, keeping a touch of its old spirit.

My father hasn't left his apartment since the renovation of the library. He refuses to come to the office holiday gathering, ignoring the invitation in his inbox that's stamped with the Department's gray seal. This season, David said he'd be handing out "famous" holiday cookies. He can't bake for shit. I've tried talking to Dad to no avail. Claire said he might just need some time alone for a bit. I don't blame him.

During lunch, I meet her in the Archive. She's cataloging Abstract Expressionism this week, photographing each canvas before they're put into climate-controlled storage. "They're calling it preservation," she says, not looking up from her computer. "Making sure art survives for future study. But you can't preserve something while killing its context." I watch her work, her movements as precise as my own drug-enhanced drafting. Her mouse clicks sound like my pills rattling. Click. Catalog. Click. Contain. Click. Control. Click. Delete.

"I saw your old professor yesterday," she mentions, finally

meeting my eyes. "Chen. He's teaching Standardized Design Principles now. Said it's better than not teaching at all." I remember Chen's classes, back when architecture was still about possibility. Now he teaches students which pre-approved template to use for which pre-defined purpose. Another kind of preservation, I suppose. The preservation of careers, of livelihoods, of people who once created but now just maintain.

The afternoon stretches into evening. Most of my colleagues leave at 5:30, their departures as coordinated as their designs. I stay late, staring at my monitor, at the perfectly acceptable Template B-244 taking shape under my regulated guidance. I don't mind working late. In fact, I enjoy the isolation. With nobody else cluttering the building, it makes my mind feel like it can wander freely. I think about my old college designs. The intricate hidden details, the curvature that guided your eyes, the essence of it all.

That's when *they* find me.

They don't introduce themselves, these twelve men and women in gray suits that match the folders they carry. They simply appear in the office, their reflections in the windows making it seem like they've surrounded me. "Malcolm Reed." one of them says – I never learn their names, never needed to. "We have an assignment for you."

Not a commission. An assignment. The word hangs in the air like smoke from a banned substance. "The Department is aware of your... extracurricular interests," another one says, placing a folder on my desk. Inside are printouts of my private sketches. The impossible buildings. The unauthorized patterns. The designs that don't fit any approved template. My old A-117

Design before I was told to "standardize" it.

I should feel afraid. Instead, I feel seen for the first time since graduation. They spread more papers across my desk – satellite photos, geological surveys, energy grid analyses. "Humanity requires a final monument," they explain. "A structure to mark the end of uncontrolled creation. Something that encapsulates everything we're leaving behind."

I don't even ask "Why me?" I know why. They chose me because I'm part of both worlds – trained in the old ways but broken to the new ones. They wanted someone impressionable and new. Somebody who was eager to work. I checked all the boxes. "Budget?" I ask instead.

"Unlimited," they say, and the word sounds like a door opening in a sealed room

I should recognize the danger in that word. Nothing unlimited exists anymore, except perhaps the capacity for control. But I'm already reaching for my sketchbook, for my pills, for the chance to build one last thing that doesn't come from a template.

The ficus shadows dance across the papers they've brought, forming patterns that look like warnings. I ignore them. Some warnings come too late to matter.

January

A couple weeks later, I've never felt more alive. Every day, I wake up before the sun, my head brimming with ideas that demand to be put to paper. I don't even bother with coffee anymore, even though Claire still offers; the sheer thrill of this project fuels me better than caffeine ever could. My sketchbook is already filled with half-finished ideas—arches that fold like waves, towers spiraling endlessly, and bridges that defy gravity. Every one of them feels like a secret pulled from the marrow of my soul.

I'm free. Truly free. No templates. No rigid guidelines. No dull gray suits standing over my shoulder, waiting to tell me I'm "off course." For the first time, I'm designing for me. I don't have to hide anything.

"Unlimited." The word still echoes in my mind, a spark that ignites every time I think about it. No budget. No restrictions. Unlimited space, unlimited resources, unlimited potential. How could I fail with that?

The days blur together in the best way. My desk is chaos— pages of sketches scattered everywhere, some with smudged charcoal streaks, others with vibrant ink splashes. I don't organize them because I don't need to. Organization is for people who follow rules, and rules don't apply to me anymore.

Even the ficus in the corner seems to approve. Its leaves have turned a brighter shade of green since I moved it closer to the window, and its shadow stretches across the floor like it's reaching for my blueprints. Sometimes I catch myself staring at those shadows, watching how they ripple and shift, like the patterns are trying to tell me something. But I'm too busy to listen. Because this is what I was made for. Not Template B-244 or standardized designs or perfectly aligned windows. I was made to create, to build, to push the boundaries of what architecture can be. And this monument—it won't just mark the end of one of humanity's eras. It will be a testament to everything we are, everything we've done, everything we could have been.

I've already begun prototyping pieces in my apartment. Faux marble columns that twist like smoke, steel beams that arc into impossible curves, glass panels that catch the light just so. I run my hands over the materials, imagining how they'll feel when they're finally assembled. My designs demand perfection, and for once, I have the resources to achieve it.

The Department hasn't bothered me since that first visit, and I take it as a sign they trust me. How could they not? They chose me, after all. Out of everyone, I'm the one who understands how to marry the old ways with the new. I can make something timeless, something immortal. My head hasn't stopped spinning since I was given this opportunity. Some nights, I don't even go home. The office becomes my sanctuary, the flickering light of my monitor the only companion I need. The silence here feels alive, like it's holding its breath, waiting to see what I'll create next. I never knew work could feel like this—like a drug, like a fever, like falling in love.

I know the risks. I know what they've given me could be a

trap, a test, a cruel joke. But I don't care. The euphoria drowns out the warnings. The ficus shadows might still be trying to tell me something, but I've stopped looking. Some warnings don't matter when you're flying this high.

Every time I walk into the studio now, it feels less like an office and more like the inside of my own mind—messy, unpredictable, alive. Drafts are pinned to the walls, overlapping and chaotic, their edges curling from the humid breath of the air conditioning. Models—some half-finished, some barely started—litter the shelves and desks, towers of plaster and steel wire reaching into nothing. There's no order to it, but it's perfect. It's mine.

I've taken to talking to the ficus. I don't even realize I'm doing it most of the time. "What do you think about this curve?" I'll ask, holding up a sketch, turning it to catch the light. "Too derivative? Or just enough to make it feel eternal?" The ficus doesn't answer, obviously, but its leaves sway faintly when the vent kicks on, like it's nodding.

I've been experimenting with materials lately, diving into the samples the Department sent. They gave me everything—stone from the mountains, reclaimed wood from ancient forests, alloys that shimmer like oil slicks in the light. Sometimes I just sit and run my fingers over the textures, imagining how they'll feel at scale. Will people touch this monument, or will they just look at it? Should it invite interaction, or demand reverence?

I've even started toying with new composites, blending materials in ways that shouldn't work but do. Yesterday, I melted shards of obsidian into clear resin and poured it into a mold shaped like a wave. The result gleamed under the studio lights, the black veins catching every flicker of motion. It was beautiful, useless, perfect.

And yet, for all this work, I still don't know what the monument will actually look like. It feels close, like I'm circling it in my mind, but every time I think I've grasped it, it shifts. Some days, I'm convinced it'll be a towering structure, something that scrapes the clouds and makes you crane your neck just to see the top. Other days, I think it should be something small, almost imperceptible, a quiet marker that forces you to pause and notice.

But I can't decide.

Not that it matters. I have time—unlimited time, or at least that's what I tell myself. The Department hasn't checked in since that first visit, and the silence only fuels my sense of invincibility. No deadlines, no parameters, no restrictions. Just me and this impossible task.

The euphoria hasn't let up. If anything, it's getting stronger. My mind feels like it's running on pure adrenaline, every moment brimming with possibility. I barely sleep anymore, maybe three or four hours at a time, but it doesn't bother me. Sleep feels like a waste when I could be creating. Last night, I dreamt about the monument. Or maybe it wasn't a dream—I was in the studio, sketching, when I must have nodded off at my desk. In the dream, or whatever it was, I was standing in front of it. The details were blurred, like looking at something underwater, but I could feel its presence. It was enormous, towering over me, yet somehow soft, inviting. I woke up with my hand still holding the pen, a jagged line scrawled across the page. I've been trying to recreate that feeling ever since.

Yet, there's a part of me that wonders if this is what they wanted. If they knew this project would consume me, that it would dig into my brain and set up camp there. But even if they did, I don't care. Let it consume me. This is what I've been waiting for my entire life—a chance to create something that matters.

The ficus's shadow stretches long across the room as the sun dips behind the skyline. I pause for the first time all day, leaning back in my chair and staring at the mess around me. Papers, models, shards of resin, scraps of metal—chaos, but it feels right. The shadow of the ficus ripples across one of the sketches, distorting the lines into something new, something I didn't intend.

It's beautiful.

I grab my pen and start sketching again just as Claire shows up unannounced, as she always does. I hear her before I see her—the unmistakable rhythm of boots against cheap office floor-tile, too loud for the office's usual hush. By the time she's at the door, I barely have time to shuffle the chaos on my desk into something resembling order. She leans against the frame, arms crossed, her smirk a perfect blend of amusement and disapproval.

"So this is where the magic happens."

I glance at the stacks of sketches, the half-finished models, I haven't talked much to Claire since they gave me this project – not because I didn't want to, but more because I just haven't had the time. I haven't made the time..

"Magic's a strong word," I say, leaning back in my chair.

Claire steps into the room, her movements slow, deliberate, like she's trying to take it all in. Her eyes flick from the plaster models to the obsidian-resin wave still drying on the corner table. "Malcolm Reed, king of chaos," she says, poking at a precariously stacked pile of blueprints. "I half expected to find you passed out in here."

"Almost did last night," I admit.

"Of course you did." She walks over to the ficus and inspects it like it might hold some secret to the madness. "You're spiraling, you know."

"I'm thriving," I correct her.

She turns, raising an eyebrow. "Is that what we're calling it now?"

Claire and I have been friends long enough for me to know when she's about to deliver a lecture disguised as a joke. But I don't have the energy to stop her—not when I know she's probably right. Instead, I hand her one of the sketches I've been working on—a towering structure that curves upward like a spiral galaxy frozen mid-spin. "What do you think?"

She studies it for a long moment, tilting her head like she's trying to see it from every angle. "Looks like a seashell on steroids."

"Exactly," I say, grinning.

Claire rolls her eyes but doesn't hand the sketch back. She folds it carefully and tucks it into her bag, like she's decided to keep it. "You're gonna need more than seashells if you want this thing to mean something."

"It's not about meaning," I argue. "It's about capturing everything we are. Everything we've built, everything we've destroyed, everything we're leaving behind."

"Sounds exhausting," she says, plopping into the chair across from me. "Maybe that's why you look like you haven't slept in three days."

"Two and a half," I mutter, rubbing my eyes.

Claire doesn't say anything for a while, just sits there, watching me like she's trying to figure out what's going on in my head. Finally, she sighs. "You know, most people would kill for this kind of freedom. Unlimited budget, no rules, no one breathing down your neck."

"Exactly," I say, leaning forward. "This is everything I've ever wanted."

"Then why do you look like you're drowning?"

The question catches me off guard. I open my mouth to answer, but nothing comes out. It's not that I'm drowning—I'm not. It's just… there's so much. Too much, maybe. Every time I think I've found the monument's shape, its essence, it slips away. Claire must see something on my face because she doesn't press. Instead, she stands and brushes imaginary crumbs off her jeans. "Come on," she says, grabbing her bag.

"Come on, where?"

"You've been cooped up in here for God knows how long," she says, gesturing to the room like it's some kind of prison cell. "Let's get out of here. Fresh air. Food that isn't whatever vending machine crap you've been living off of."

"I don't have time," I start, but she cuts me off.

"You have all the time in the world, remember?" she says, throwing my own words back at me. "Unlimited, or whatever."

I hesitate, glancing at the papers spread across my desk. She's right. And if I'm being honest, the idea of stepping outside this room, even for a little while, is starting to sound appealing.

"Fine," I say, standing. "But you're paying."

"Obviously," Claire says, grinning as she heads for the door. I take my first lunch break in days.

The diner Claire drags me to is the kind of place that smells like burnt coffee and grease but somehow manages to feel comforting anyway. It's late enough that the dinner rush is long gone, and the few remaining customers are scattered across booths like weary travelers clinging to their cups of coffee. It looks like it used to be a retro-themed 'Mom & Pop' shop before the Renovations.

Claire slides into a booth by the window without waiting for me, tossing her bag into the seat beside her. "Order something that doesn't come in a wrapper," she says, already scanning the menu.

I sit across from her and glance out the window. The neon sign outside casts a cool white glow over the glass, making everything feel a little surreal. A little dystopian. It almost reminds me of the nights back in college when we'd pull all-nighters and reward ourselves with greasy food at places just like this.

Except this isn't college anymore, and there's no exam or project deadline waiting to slap me back to reality. The only thing waiting for me is the monument.

"You're thinking about it, aren't you?" Claire says, not even looking up from the menu.

"About what?"

"The project. The monument. Whatever you're calling it in your head."

"Maybe," I admit.

"Mal," she says, finally meeting my eyes. "You need to chill."

"I am relaxed," I say, leaning back in the booth.

She raises an eyebrow. "Sure you are. That's why you're vibrating with whatever manic energy you've got going on."

I open my mouth to argue, but the waitress arrives before I can say anything. Claire orders pancakes and bacon—her go-to comfort food—and I get a burger, even though I'm not really hungry.

When the waitress leaves, Claire leans forward, resting her chin on her hand. "Look, I get it," she says. "This is your dream project. You've been waiting your whole life for something like this. But if you keep letting it chew you up like this, it's going to win. And I don't think you want that."

"I'm not letting it win," I say, maybe a little too defensively. "It's important," I say.

"I know it is," she says, her voice softer now. "But you can't carry the weight of the whole world on your shoulders, Malcolm. Not even you."

I want to tell her she's wrong, that I can handle it, that I have to handle it. But the words stick in my throat, and instead, I just sit there, staring at the salt shaker on the table.

When the food comes, Claire doesn't press the issue. She just eats her pancakes, occasionally offering a running commentary on the diner's decor.

It's comforting in a way I didn't realize I needed.

By the time we leave, I feel lighter, like some of the weight in my chest has been siphoned off. Claire doesn't say anything as we walk back to the car, but when we stop at a crosswalk, she bumps my shoulder with hers.

I return to the office later that night, but I swear the room feels different. Not quieter, exactly, but calmer. Like it's waiting for me to catch my breath.

I drop into my chair, glance at the chaos on my desk, and pick up the sketch I started before Claire showed up. It's rough, incomplete, but the bones of something extraordinary are there. My euphoria builds back up. I let it.

I work until my internal clock says stop. These days, that time is around 1:30 AM. I leave for the day just to come back and do it all again. Yet, I don't feel the dread that I use to feel every day. Back when David would tell me my window alignments were off.

The next morning, I wake to the sound of my alarm blaring at full volume. I barely wake up and get ready to rush out the door for work. I feel like I'm the only person to want to go to work this badly. The excitement from last night hasn't dulled. If anything, it's stronger now, buzzing under my skin like caffeine. I grab my bag, shove the sketchbook inside, and head out the door, barely noticing the faint sunlight creeping through my window.

By the time I get to the office, I'm already running on adrenaline.

"No coffee?" Claire asks, holding up her own mug like it's the holy grail. "Who are you, and what have you done with Malcolm?"

"Don't need it," I say, pulling out my sketchbook. "Look at this."

She sets her mug down and leans over the table, her eyes scanning the page. For a moment, she says nothing, her expression unreadable.

"It's… chaotic," she says finally, though there's no malice in her tone.

"It's a start," I say, flipping to another page where I've started mapping out dimensions. "I was thinking about using a spiral foundation, something that feels organic but also deliberate. Something that pulls you in, makes you feel like you're part of it."

Claire sits back, crossing her arms. "Part of what?"

I hesitate, searching for the right words. "Part of… everything. The history, the progress, the mistakes. All of it."

"Something like Dad's library?," she asks, but there's a hint of a smile on her lips.

"Exactly." I say, unable to keep the grin off my face.

She watches me for a moment, like she's trying to decide whether to encourage me or call me insane. Eventually, she picks up her coffee and takes a long sip. "Well, if anyone's crazy enough to pull it off, it's you."

"Thanks, I think."

The rest of the day passes in a blur of ideas and revisions. I throw myself into the work, sketching, drafting, scrapping, and starting over again. The euphoria hasn't faded—it's like a drug, keeping me focused and sharp.

But even in my most productive moments, Claire's words from the diner linger in the back of my mind. You can't carry the weight of the whole world on your shoulders.

I push the thought aside, telling myself I'll worry about it later. For now, there's too much to do, too much to create. I'm beginning to feel like I'm not alone in this. And for now, that's enough.

By the end of the week, my desk is a battlefield. Crumpled sketches litter the floor like casualties of war, and my monitor blinks with half-finished models that feel more like compromises than triumphs. The euphoria that kept me afloat earlier in the week has dulled into something heavier, harder to carry.

I've been running on fumes, and it's starting to show.

February

It's February now, and the glow of January's freedom has dulled. At first, I'd stopped taking the pills altogether. The creative high I felt after ditching the templates was intoxicating enough on its own. For the first time in years, I didn't need Adderall to power through another soul-sucking, standardized design. The freedom to build something truly mine had been better than any chemical rush.

But it didn't last.

A month ago, my ideas flowed like water. Now they trickle. Some days, they don't come at all. The monument looms larger and more impossible with every sketch I throw away. I used to relish the blank page; now it stares back at me like a silent accusation. My head feels like a clogged drain—there's pressure, but nothing moves.

The first time I reached for the bottle again, it was after a particularly brutal night. I'd been staring at the same page for hours, pencil hovering uselessly above the paper. I told myself it was just for tonight. Just one pill to clear my head, to remind myself what focus felt like.

Now, one pill is part of my morning routine. Sometimes, it's two.

The February sunlight streams through the office window

as I sit at my desk, sketchpad open in front of me. The ficus casts jagged shadows across the paper, and I can't help but feel like they're mocking me. I shake the bottle in my hand—once, twice—before tilting it and letting a pill fall into my palm.

The ritual is so familiar now that I don't even think about it. The pill goes down dry, bitter and chalky against my tongue. I wash it down with a swig of cold coffee, and within minutes, my chest starts to loosen, my thoughts sharpening into clarity. The jittery, overstimulated edge will come later, but for now, the rush feels clean.

I press my pencil to the paper, and for the first time in days, the lines come easily.

"Good morning," Claire's voice startles me out of my focus. She's leaning against the doorframe, her coffee mug cradled in one hand.

"Morning," I reply without looking up. My hand keeps moving, the adrenaline from the pill driving me to get as much done as I can before the crash inevitably comes.

"Working hard?" she asks, stepping inside.

"Always."

She snorts. "You look like hell, Malcolm. When's the last time you went home?"

"Last night," I lie.

She raises an eyebrow, unconvinced. "Right. And how much of that time did you spend asleep?"

I don't answer. Instead, I flip to another page in my sketchbook and start on a new angle of the monument.

"Okay, keep your secrets." She perches on the edge of my desk, peering down at my sketchpad. "How's the masterpiece coming along?"

"It's getting there," I mutter.

Claire studies the lines on the page, her lips pursed. "It's good," she says finally. "But…"

"But what?"

She hesitates, then shrugs. "I don't know. It's missing something. Like… it's too perfect, if that makes sense."

I laugh, a short, sharp sound that surprises even me. "Too perfect. Great. I'll be sure to fuck it up for you."

"That's not what I meant," she says, frowning. "I just—"

"You just what?" I snap, the irritation bubbling up before I can stop it.

She raises her hands in mock surrender. "Okay, okay. Touchy subject. Forget I said anything."

She hops off the desk and heads for the door, pausing to glance back at me. "Just don't burn yourself out again, okay? This place is lonely when you're passed out under the ficus."

Her words hang in the air after she leaves, but I don't let them stick. I pop another pill and get back to work.

The rush comes fast, and the monument starts to take shape again. I sketch with a kind of manic precision, the lines on the page perfectly crisp, perfectly ordered.

But Claire's right.

It is too perfect. And I have no idea how to fix it.

The second pill doesn't hit quite like the first. It never does. The clarity it gives me is sharp, but it cuts differently now, leaving behind an edge I can't dull. My heart feels like it's keeping pace with my pencil, each beat a quick thud that matches the rhythm of my frantic sketching.

I lean back in my chair, staring at the newest draft. It's clean, flawless, and lifeless. Claire's voice rings in my head: *"It's missing something."*

I hate that she's right.

The monument, as it stands now, could win awards, grace whatever magazines are still in production, maybe even last through the ages. But it's sterile. It doesn't *feel* like anything. It's just lines and angles and symmetry, another monument to perfectionism rather than humanity. And yet, I can't stop sketching it this way. My brain won't let me.

The bottle sits next to my coffee cup. I think about taking another pill, then shake my head. "Get it together, Malcolm," I mutter under my breath.

Instead, I grab my jacket and step outside.

The February air bites at my face, sharp and cold, a slap of reality that I desperately need. The city feels different in the winter, quieter somehow. There's a thin layer of frost clinging to the edges of buildings, their sterile exteriors blending into the gray sky. I walk without a destination, hoping that moving my legs will jog my brain into some kind of clarity.

I find myself at Dad's old library. Its façade is new and ugly in a way only perfection can be.

But the bones of the place are still the same. I run my fingers along the edge of a concrete bench out front, its surface cold enough to sting. It's not like the old benches, the ones with chipped paint and worn wood that told stories of the people who sat there. This one is just… functional.

Like my monument.

I sit down, pulling my sketchpad from under my arm. The ideas come, but they're rushed, forced. Each line feels like it's trying too hard to matter, to mean something. The pencil snaps in my hand, and I curse under my breath.

"You okay there, champ?"

I glance up to see Claire standing in front of me, bundled in a long coat, a scarf wrapped loosely around her neck. She's holding a steaming coffee cup in one hand and a small paper bag in the other.

"What are you doing here?" I ask, shoving the broken pencil into my pocket.

"Looking for you, obviously. Thought you might've collapsed in a snowbank somewhere." She hands me the bag. "Eat."

I open it to find a stale-looking croissant. "Thanks for the gourmet meal."

"Hey, it's better than whatever vending machine crap you've been living off of."

I take a bite, more out of obligation than hunger. "So what, you just decided to stalk me?"

"I prefer to think of it as *concerned observation*." She sits next to me, her breath visible in the cold air. "You've been a ghost lately, Malcolm. Even for you."

"I've been busy," I say, brushing crumbs off my lap.

"You mean you've been avoiding people." She sips her coffee, her gaze fixed on the horizon. "You can't keep doing this to yourself, you know. Burning the candle at both ends, popping pills like they're vitamins. It's not sustainable."

I laugh bitterly. "Claire, this entire project isn't sustainable. I'm trying to build something to represent humanity's legacy, and I can't even figure out what *humanity* is supposed to look like anymore."

She turns to face me, her expression softer than I expect. "You know, maybe that's the point."

"What is?"

"That it doesn't have to be perfect. Humanity isn't perfect. Maybe your monument shouldn't be, either."

I want to dismiss her, to wave away her words as naïve, but I can't. She has a way of cutting through my bullshit, always has.

"I don't know how to *not* make it perfect," I admit quietly.

She smiles, a small, almost sad smile. "That's the Malcolm Reed I know. Always fighting himself, even when he doesn't need to."

The wind picks up, and I pull my jacket tighter around me. For a moment, we sit in silence, watching the city move around us.

"You should come back to the office," she says finally. "But only if you promise to take a break every once in a while."

"Yeah," I say, though I don't mean it.

Claire rolls her eyes but stands anyway, brushing snow off her coat. "Just… don't forget why you started this, okay? It wasn't about proving anything to anyone."

I nod, watching her walk away.

But even as I sit there, trying to absorb her words, my hand is already itching to reach for my sketchpad again.

By the time I get back to my apartment, it's dark outside, and the city looks like a blueprint—cold, calculated, and lifeless. I drop my sketchpad on the kitchen counter and immediately regret it when I hear the crunch of paper bending under its own weight. My fingers twitch, instinctively reaching for the Adderall bottle before I stop myself.

I replay Claire's words in my head. Its like she holds some sort of power over me nobody else can. I don't need it.

I pull open the fridge instead, staring blankly at its contents. A carton of eggs I haven't touched. A loaf of bread with just enough mold creeping on the edges to make me question it. Coffee creamer. Cottage cheese. There's no actual food here, and I can't even pretend to be surprised.

I grab a can of something microwavable from the pantry and plop onto the couch. The microwave whirs behind me, but my mind is somewhere else—back at the library bench. Back to that conversation with Claire.

The thing is, Claire's wrong. Or at least, I want her to be.

This monument has to be perfect. It has to mean *something*. Otherwise, it's just another fucking building. And if I can't even design that right, what's the point?

The microwave beeps, and I ignore it.

I crack open my laptop, fully intending to keep working, but instead, I find myself scrolling through old photos I haven't looked at in years. College parties. The road trip to New Orleans. I linger on that one for a moment longer than the others. I need to get out.

Maybe somewhere like Rome.

I think to myself about how I wasn't always like this. There was a time when I didn't measure my worth in perfectly aligned sketches and impossible deadlines. A time when I didn't need a pill to push me through every single day.

But then I remember why I started taking them in the first place.

It wasn't just the guidelines, the bureaucracy, the endless meetings where every good idea got flattened into mediocrity. It was the exhaustion. The suffocating weight of knowing that no matter what I did, it would never be enough. Not for the Department. Not for my colleagues. Not even for myself.

The pills made it easier. They turned the noise into clarity, the chaos into focus. And now, without them, the noise is creeping back in.

I slam the laptop shut, pushing it away like it's offended me somehow. My eyes flick to the bottle on the counter.

Fuck.

I don't need it.

But the thought doesn't leave me alone.

Instead, it nags at me, whispering the same thing over and over: *Just one. Just enough to get through the night. Just enough to stop the noise.*

I stand up, pacing the tiny living room like a caged animal.

I grab the bottle, shaking it lightly. The pills rattle like a countdown.

I unscrew the cap and stare at the tiny orange tablets inside. One won't hurt. It's not like I'm going to spiral into addiction overnight. I'm smarter than that. More disciplined.

Right?

But I don't take one. Not yet. Instead, I leave the bottle open on the counter and sit back down on the couch.

The next morning, the bottle is still sitting on the counter, wide open, the pills gleaming under the pale light of the kitchen. I stare at it like it's a loaded gun.

I barely slept last night. Not because I was working late—no, the sketchpad remained untouched—but because my mind wouldn't shut up. It felt like I was hosting a fucking panel discussion of every self-doubt, every half-baked thought, and every unfinished idea that had ever crossed my mind. By 3 a.m., I was convinced the monument was a mistake, that I was a mistake.

By 6 a.m., I wasn't convinced of anything at all.

I grab a mug and pour myself a cup of coffee. It's black and bitter and tastes like regret.

I remember my food still in the microwave.

Claire texts me sometime soon after.

"Lunch later?"

It sounds much more appetizing. I leave for work and leave the pills on the counter.

I make it inside by seven. Work goes by slow but by lunchtime, I'm sitting in the break room with a cup of instant noodles, half-listening to my coworkers discuss some new regulations on resource allocation. I don't say anything, too lost in my own thoughts to bother joining the conversation.

My phone buzzes again. Another text from Claire.

"Still alive?"

"Barely," I type back, forcing a half-smile.

Her response comes almost immediately.

"I'm on my way :)" She types from the Archives downstairs.

I stare at the screen for a moment before replying.

"Sure."

Claire has a way of pulling me back from the edge, even when I don't want to be saved.

March

March arrives in pieces.

The city wakes up, shaking off its winter coat, and for a moment—just a moment—you forget it's a place built on order. The trees lining the streets bloom with an audacity that feels almost rebellious. Yellow forsythia bursts from the cracks in the sidewalks, their roots twisting against the gray slabs like clenched fists. Even the air smells brighter, alive with that faint metallic hint of rain yet to come.

But the gray is still there, stretched over everything like an unwashed blanket, dulling the edges of the world. It's not the kind of gray that storms; it's the kind that lingers, that clings to your skin and your thoughts.

I wish I could rip it off, like Claire can tear the dust covers off my brain. She'd probably say something snarky about that, too, if she were here,

The truth is, I've felt different this month. Calmer, maybe. Sharper, even. My head doesn't feel like it's clawing at itself anymore, desperate for clarity. But the absence of pills isn't exactly a relief—it's more like standing on a high ledge after someone's removed the railing.

I miss the edge it gave me. The clean, single-minded focus. That rush of feeling like I could take on anything. But now, without it, I don't feel burnt out anymore. My mind feels like it belongs to me again.

And that terrifies me.

Claire finds me sitting on the steps of the park fountain, the concrete still cool from what's left of winter. My sketchbook lays open but untouched. The monument sketches have stalled again, caught somewhere between "unfinished" and "overthought," and I've been coming here to try and push through it.

"You're brooding," she says, handing me a coffee cup that's still too hot to touch.

"Just thinking," I reply, though the way she looks at me says she knows that's bullshit.

Claire sits down next to me, close enough that our shoulders almost touch but not quite. She's got one of those Patagonia windbreaker jackets on, bright orange against the muted cityscape, like she's daring the gray to swallow her whole. I've never seen anybody pull off a bright orange windbreaker as well as she is now.

"Sketches still giving you hell?" she asks, nodding toward the book in my lap.

"Something like that."

"You know," she says, taking a sip of her coffee, "you're allowed to just... I don't know... stop overthinking and do something completely stupid."

"Isn't that what got me into this mess in the first place?" I smirk, flipping the book shut.

"That's different," she says, grinning. "Your 'stupid' is actually interesting. The rest of us just settle for functional."

I laugh, despite myself.

The fountain burbles beside us, its sound cutting through

the city's white noise. For a moment, we don't talk. I let the quiet fill the space between us, let the smell of damp stone and blooming flowers remind me that the world is still moving, whether I'm ready for it or not.

"What if it's not enough?" I ask suddenly, surprising even myself.

Claire doesn't ask what I mean. She just tilts her head slightly, her gaze thoughtful but sharp.

"It doesn't have to be enough," she says after a moment. "It just has to be yours."

The words settle into my chest, soft but heavy.

"Do you want me to leave you to brood in peace?" she adds, already getting to her feet.

"No," I say, standing too. "Let's walk."

She doesn't ask where, and I don't tell her. Sometimes it's easier that way, letting the city decide the direction for you.

The short walk turns into hours of wondering. The city guides us with every street corner. Claire doesn't say much and neither do I. I enjoy her company and I think she enjoyed mine.

By the time we part ways, the sun is setting, throwing streaks of orange and gold across the horizon. I watch her walk away, her windbreaker blending in with the sky.

Back in my apartment, I open the sketchbook again, and for once, the blank page doesn't feel like a challenge.

Spring is here, and I don't feel tired anymore. That feels like something worth building on.

The air smells like earth again. Not processed, or filtered, or unnatural, but the real thing—the damp, mineral smell of soil waking up from winter.

I have a lot of time to self-reflect on these mornings. I think about my childhood often. I think about my birthday coming up. I think about all the family traditions we used to have. I don't celebrate any of it anymore. Not because I'm depressed or because I hate being happy, it just isn't the same as it was before. Claire's birthday is sometime in September, I think. I wonder if she celebrates it.

I take the long way to the office the next morning, passing rows of cherry blossoms that haven't quite bloomed yet. Their buds are clenched tight, waiting for some invisible signal. I envy them, in a way. They know exactly when to open, when to let go.

I step into my office, sketchbook tucked under my arm, and let myself breathe it all in. For the first time in weeks, I don't feel the itch to reach for anything—no pills, no coffee, not even my pen. I just stand there, staring at what I've built so far.

Claire shows up an hour later, carrying a bag of pastries that smell like heaven and look like they've been through hell.

"They had a two-for-one deal on croissants," she says, handing me one that's slightly smooshed. "Don't say I never did anything for you."

I take it without comment, because you don't question free pastries, no matter how beat up they are.

"Shouldn't you be at work?" I ask, brushing a flake of pastry off my jacket.

"Shouldn't *you* be at work?" she counters, raising an eyebrow.

"This is work."

She glances at the monument behind me, her expression somewhere between impressed and skeptical. "You're really going for it, huh?"

"That's the job," I say, taking a bite of the croissant. It's stale, but I don't care.

Claire leans against the wall, crossing her arms. "You don't seem as… jittery as usual. No offense."

"None taken," I say, though the comment sticks in my head. "I've been cutting back."

"On the pills?"

I nod, swallowing a mouthful of croissant that feels like it's mostly air. "Stopped completely a little bit ago."

"Wow," she says, genuinely surprised. "So, what's it like being free of the corporate speed machine?"

I shrug, though I know the answer. It's like taking off a pair of glasses you didn't know you were wearing. Everything looks softer, less sharp. Less urgent.

"Feels weird," I admit.

Claire snorts. "You're weird."

That alone is enough to make me laugh. She grins at that.

"Come on," she says, tossing the rest of her pastry into the trash can. "Show me what you've got so far."

We walk the perimeter of the office-turned-studio, Claire picking her way through the discarded paper on the floor. She stops every so often to ask questions—about the angles, the materials, the way the light will hit the surfaces once it's finished.

She's not an architect, but she sees things I don't.

"That curve there," she says, pointing to one of the support beams in a design of mine. "It's too soft. Makes the whole thing feel… I don't know. Passive."

"Passive?" I repeat, frowning.

"Yeah," she says, motioning with her hands. "It's like you're trying to make something bold, but then you second-guessed yourself halfway through."

I hate that she's right. She always is it seems. I envy it.

"Passive," I mutter, making a note in the margin of my

sketchbook.

Claire watches me scribble, her arms crossed again. "You're really taking this seriously, huh?"

"What, you thought I wouldn't?"

She shrugs. "I don't know. You used to be so… checked out all the time. It's weird seeing you actually care about something."

"I always cared," I say, though it comes out defensive. "I just didn't have anything worth caring about."

Claire doesn't say anything to that. She just watches me for a moment, her expression unreadable.

"Alright," she says finally. "Let's see if you can make it un-passive, or whatever."

"Bold," I correct.

"Bold," she echoes, smirking.

By the time she leaves, my office is buzzing with creativity. I stay longer than I planned, pacing the workplace with my sketchbook, tweaking angles and curves, trying to make everything just a little less 'passive.'

When I finally head home, the city feels brighter somehow. The cherry blossoms are still closed, but their promise hangs in the air, carried on the wind like a whispered secret. For the first time in months, I feel like I'm moving forward.

Yet, my mind isn't clear. I think of my dad. His voice lingers in my head. I think about him when I try to go to sleep, my thoughts seeming to drift back to him. To the way his voice sounded the last time I talked to him—thinner, like something was wearing him down. I should see him.

Then, there's a knock at the door, echoing through my apartment.

I hesitate for a moment before standing, the weight of my thoughts slowing me down. When I open the door, Claire is there, holding a bottle of wine and harboring a lopsided grin.

"Figured I could surprise you with a break," she says, brushing past me into the apartment like she lives here.

"Claire," I start, closing the door behind her. "It's late."

"Relax," she says, kicking off her shoes and heading straight for the kitchen. "I'm not here to interrogate you. I just thought, you know, you've been doing great with the project, and maybe it's time to celebrate a little."

I force a smile, but my chest feels tight. "I'm not really in the mood."

She doesn't seem to hear me. She's already pulling two glasses from my cabinet, pouring the wine like it's a normal Tuesday night and not… whatever this is.

"You've been killing it, Malcolm," she says, handing me a glass. "The project, the sketches—it's like you're finally waking up again. It's good to see."

I take the glass but don't drink. "Thanks."

I take a seat on the couch, she follows but doesn't sit.

Her smile falters slightly. "Come on, you don't seem happy. What's wrong?"

"It's nothing," I say quickly. "I'm just tired."

She sets her glass down and crosses her arms. "Bullshit. You've been tired for years, Malcolm. This is different."

I sigh, running a hand through my hair. "It's my dad."

"What about him?"

I pause, unsure how much I want to share. "He's not doing well. His health… it's been bad for a while now."

She nods slowly, her expression softening. "I'm sorry. I didn't know."

"It's fine," I say, even though it's not. "I just… I've got a lot on my mind right now."

She steps closer and puts her hand on my chest, her voice gentles. "Maybe I can help."

Her words hang in the air, and for a moment, I want to let her in. I want to tell her everything, show her everything, show her all of me, I want to lean on her the way she's leaned on me. But then I see her standing there, so sure of herself, and it just feels too weighing.

"Claire, I can't do this right now," I say, setting the glass down.

Her brow furrows. "Do what?"

"This." I gesture vaguely between us. "Whatever you're trying to make this into."

Her face hardens. "I'm trying to be here for you, Malcolm. Is that such a bad thing?"

"No, but—"

"But what?"

I suddenly feel cornered. "I don't know, Claire. It's just not a good time."

Her voice sharpens. "When is a good time, then? Because it seems like every time I try to get close, you push me away."

"That's not fair."

"No, Malcolm, what's not fair is you acting like I'm some background character in your little genius narrative. I'm your friend. I've been here for you since the beginning of this and now it's like I don't even know who you are anymore."

Her words hit harder than I expect, and for a moment, I can't think of a response.

She shakes her head, her voice softer now but no less cutting. "You're so focused on everyone else's expectations, you don't even see what's right in front of you."

I glare at her, the frustration boiling over. "You don't get it, Claire. You don't know what it's like to feel like you're failing everyone—your dad, your work, yourself. So don't stand there and act like you do."

Her eyes narrow, and I know I've gone too far.

"You're right," she says quietly. "I don't know what it's like. But maybe if you let someone in for once, you wouldn't have to carry it alone."

I stand up and face her. "You don't get it, Claire. This isn't just some project to me. This is my chance to do something real, something without all the rules and restrictions we've been drowning in. It's the first thing in years that feels like mine."

"And that's great," she says, her voice rising now. "But at what cost? You're shutting everyone out, Malcolm. You've been so focused on this damn monument that you've turned into—"

"Turned into what?" I interrupt, my voice sharp enough to make her stop. "Say it."

"A fucking robot," she says, the words hanging in the air like smoke. "You're obsessed, Malcolm. It's like you've replaced one set of rules with another, and you're too blind to see it."

The room goes silent except for the faint hum of the heater. I stare at her, my hands clenched into fists at my sides, and I can't decide if I'm angry because she's wrong or because she might be right.

She grabs her shoes and heads for the door, her movements sharp and deliberate.

"Claire—"

"Goodnight, Malcolm," she says without looking back.

The door slams shut, and I'm left standing there, the room feeling emptier than it did before she arrived.

The silence is deafening.

The wine glass sits untouched on the counter, but I don't have the energy to put it away. Instead, I sink onto the couch, my head in my hands.

For all the progress I've made, it feels like I'm still stuck in the same damn place.

I don't see Claire for a while after that.

She doesn't come by my office, doesn't call, doesn't even text. At first, I tell myself it's fine. I'm busy anyway, too wrapped up in the project to worry about anything else. Besides, what did I do wrong? But as the days go by, her absence starts to feel like a hole I can't ignore.

The monument is progressing faster than I expected. It should feel like progress, but instead, it feels hollow.

I tell myself it's just the stress, the pressure of getting everything right. I bury myself more and more in the work, pouring over blueprints and sketches, tweaking details that no one but me will notice. But no matter how much I do, it doesn't feel like enough.

One night, I find myself staring at the ficus tree in the corner of my office again. Its leaves are glossy and green, its branches stretching toward the light like it knows exactly where it's going. I envy its certainty, its quiet resilience.

I think about calling Claire.

I pick up my phone, my thumb hovering over her name in my contacts list. But what would I even say? Sorry I've been a dick?

I put the phone back in my pocket.

I find myself on my father's nursing home's porch later that evening after work, the spring air sticking to my skin like an unwelcome reminder that things are supposed to feel lighter this time of year. The trees are beginning to bloom, their pink and white blossoms scattered like confetti on the pavement. The air outside smells alive—fresh cut grass, warm dirt, the faint tang of citrus from somewhere I can't pinpoint.

But the assisted-living home feels the opposite. The sickening bland walls and straight edges. It's a minimalist's dream in a nightmare.

I walk past reception. The air smells sterile now. My dad's apartment door is open and I walk in. A cup of tea rests on his table, steam curling lazily in the air. He looks thinner than the last time I saw him, the lines on his face cutting deeper into his skin.

"You look like hell," he says, not bothering to glance up from his newspaper.

"Nice to see you too," I reply, easing into the chair beside him.

He folds the paper in half with deliberate slowness, sets it on the little table between us, and finally looks at me. His eyes linger just a second too long, like he's assessing something he's not ready to say out loud.

"You don't usually come by on weekdays," he says.

"Maybe I wanted to check on you."

"Bullshit." He picks up his mug and takes a slow sip. "What's really going on?"

I look out at the street through his room's small standardized window, watching a kid on a bike wobble past, his helmet too big for his head. "Claire and I got into it," I admit after a long pause.

"Ah." He sets the mug down, nodding like that explains everything.

"That's it? No 'what happened'? No lecture about how I probably fucked up?"

He chuckles, a low rumble that seems to come from somewhere deep in his chest. "You already know you fucked up. Why waste my breath?"

I can't help but laugh, even though it's short and bitter. "Thanks for the vote of confidence."

"Look, Malcolm," he says, leaning back in his chair. "Arguments happen. Especially with someone like Claire. She's sharp, she doesn't take shit from anyone—including you—and she probably cares more than she lets on. That's a dangerous combination."

"Dangerous how?"

He shrugs, picking up his tea again. "Dangerous for your pride. You can't out-logic someone like her, so don't even try. She'll see through you every damn time."

"I think I said something I can't take back."

"Then don't take it back," he says simply.

"What?"

"You heard me. Don't take it back. Own it. Apologize for how you said it, maybe, but if it came out of your mouth, then there's a reason it was in your head in the first place." He pauses, giving me a pointed look. "You think she's not doing the same thing? Stewing over whatever dumbass thing she said to you?"

The thought hadn't occurred to me, and I hate how much I want it to be true.

We sit in silence for a while, the kind that only happens with someone who knows you better than you'd like. The sun dips lower in the sky, its warmth fading, and my dad starts coughing—a deep, rattling sound that makes me wince.

"You should see a doctor," I say. "An actual one. Not one of these nurses here."

"Doctors are expensive," he replies between coughs, waving me off.

"You have insurance."

"Still expensive."

I sigh, leaning forward with my elbows on my knees. "Seriously, Dad. This has been going on for months. What if it's something—"

"It's nothing," he interrupts, his tone sharp enough to cut me off. "I'm fine, Malcolm. Worry about your own damn problems."

I sit back, biting back the urge to argue. He's always been stubborn, but this feels different. He's dodging, deflecting, and I can't shake the feeling that he's hiding something.

As I leave that evening, his words linger in my mind. 'Worry about your own problems.'

If only I knew how. I kiss him bye, and head home.

Back at my apartment, I sit on the couch with a notebook balanced on my knee. Sketches and measurements sprawl across the page, but my focus keeps drifting.

My phone buzzes on the coffee table, I grab it without checking the caller ID.

"Malcolm?" It's my father's nurse, Mrs. Tran.

I sit up straighter. She never calls unless it's about something important. "Yeah? What's going on?"

"It's your father. I found him coughing in his room after you left. It didn't sound good—worse than usual. I told him to go to the doctor, but you know how he is."

I grip the phone tighter. "Did he say what it was?"

She hesitates, her voice dropping to a whisper, as if he might overhear her from in reception. "He's not saying much of anything, Malcolm. But I think it's bad. He looked... pale. Tired. Not himself."

The words settle into my chest like stones, heavy and cold.

"Thanks for letting me know," I say, my throat dry.

An hour later, I'm back in his building. The air smells damp now. His door isn't open this time. I knock once before letting myself in.

"Dad?"

I find him in the kitchen, leaning against the counter with the same mug in his hands.

"What are you doing here again?" he asks, his voice hoarse.

"Mrs. Tran called me."

His eyes narrow. "That woman needs to mind her own business."

"She's worried about you. I am too."

He sets the mug down harder than necessary, the clink of ceramic against granite breaking the tense silence. "I'm fine."

"Bullshit," I snap, surprising even myself with the force of it. "You've been coughing for months. You look like hell. Just tell me what's going on."

He stares at me, his jaw tightening. For a moment, I think he's going to brush me off again, but then he exhales slowly, like he's been holding his breath for years.

"It's my lungs," he says finally. "COPD."

The words land like a punch to the gut. I knew something was wrong, but hearing it out loud makes it real in a way I wasn't ready for.

"How long have you known?" I ask, my voice quieter now.

"A while." He shrugs, trying to look indifferent, but there's something fragile in his posture. "Doctor said it's common in people 'my age.'"

"Are you… are you getting treatment?"

"I've got an inhaler," he says, holding up the small device like it's a joke. "And some meds. Nothing fancy."

"Jesus, Dad." I run a hand through my hair, the frustration and worry tangling into a knot in my chest. "Why didn't you tell me?"

"Because you've got enough on your plate," he says simply. "I didn't want to be another thing for you to worry about."

"Yeah, well, too late for that."

We stand there in the kitchen, the sound of the rain starting to patter against the windows. I want to yell at him for being so stubborn, for hiding this from me, but I can't. He looks so damn tired, and I hate the thought of adding to his burden.

"Let me help," I say finally.

"You're helping by being here." He gives me a small, tired smile. "That's enough for now."

But it doesn't feel like enough. Not even close.

Spring is supposed to be a season of renewal, of fresh starts. But as the rain beats against his window, it feels more like a reminder that everything—people, seasons, even cities—has its limits.

And my father, for all his stubbornness, is no exception.

April

April comes with a cautious warmth, the kind that lingers in the corners of a room. It's the first time in months that I've felt the need to loosen my tie and roll up my sleeves at work. Outside, the cherry blossoms are finally blooming in defiance of the gray city, their soft pink petals clinging to the air like a stubborn reminder of beauty.

I decide to loosen up, too.

The project is still my focus, but I can't keep letting it consume me. March was a blur of late nights and strained nerves, and I don't want to feel like that again. I can't. Claire's words still haunt me, replaying when the office gets too quiet, but I haven't found the courage to face her yet. Or maybe it's the other way around.

Instead, I focus on myself, trying to peel away the layers of tension and expectation I've wrapped myself in over the years.

It starts small—leaving the office earlier, taking the long way home to walk through the park. The ficus tree in the corner of my office has sprouted new leaves, and I water it carefully, as if tending to it might somehow help me grow, too.

Work is still there, of course. It always is. But I've started drawing for myself again. Nothing big, just little sketches in the margins of my notebooks like I used to do. Curves that don't align with any standard, details that have no purpose other than to exist. I keep them to myself, hidden in the same way I used to hide my old unauthorized patterns, but this time it feels different. Lighter. Like a secret I'm willing to carry. Maybe it's because I know I can get away with having unauthorized designs in my office now, or maybe it's something entirely different. I don't know.

I see Claire sometimes, down in the archives. She's always busy, or she at least looks like it when I'm there, surrounded by rows of metal shelves and boxes that look like they haven't been touched in decades. She doesn't look up when I pass by, and I don't try to get her attention. It's easier this way, I tell myself. Less complicated.

I've taken my mind away from relationships and focused more on social life. The nostalgia for my college days brings a new sort of youthfulness to my work life.

I caught wind of a bar night from a few coworkers. I don't even remember who brought it up, just that the words hit my ears during a coffee break.

"Friday after work," one of them says. "You should come, Malcolm. It'll be fun."

Fun. I haven't thought about what that feels like in a long time.

Maybe I need this. Maybe I need to try.

"I'll think about it," I say, and the words feel like a small rebellion against myself.

By Friday, I've convinced myself to go. I tell myself it's just one evening. Just a drink or two. Just… something different. I don't want to let the project take control of me again.

The bar is one of those places that tries too hard to feel authentic. Exposed brick walls, dim lighting, vintage posters that probably cost more than the drinks. It tries so hard to not look standardized, I'm surprised my goody-two-shoes coworkers even come here. It's the kind of place I would have rolled my eyes at in college, but tonight, it doesn't bother me. It's not about the setting—it's about stepping outside of my usual routine, testing the waters of something unfamiliar.

I spot my coworkers near the back, crowded around a table littered with empty glasses and baskets of half-eaten fries. They wave me over, their smiles a little too eager, like they're surprised I actually showed up.

"Reed!" Jason, one of the junior designers, calls out. I'm not close with him at all—hell, I'm not close with anybody from the office. He's always been a little too enthusiastic for my taste, the kind of guy who organizes office birthday cards and laughs too loudly at mediocre jokes. But tonight, his energy feels less grating.

"Didn't think you'd make it," he says, sliding a chair out for me.

"I didn't either," I admit, and that gets a chuckle from the group.

The conversation is light—mostly office gossip and complaints about upper management. I find myself being able to listen without feeling the need to dissect every word, without searching for hidden motives or passive-aggressive undertones. They're not *bad* people, I realize. Just... ordinary.

A round of drinks arrives, and someone hands me a pint of something dark and bitter. I take a sip and grimace, which earns another round of laughter.

"Not a beer guy?" Jason asks, raising an eyebrow.

"Not this kind," I say, setting the glass down.

"Stick around. We'll find something you like," he says, and

it's not a promise I expect him to keep, but it feels nice to hear anyway.

I start to relax as the night goes on. The alcohol helps, of course, but it's more than that. There's a rhythm to the conversation, a back-and-forth that reminds me of late nights in college dorms, the kind of easy camaraderie I haven't felt in years.

Someone suggests a game of darts, and I surprise myself once again by agreeing to join. I'm terrible at it—my aim is laughably off—but nobody seems to care. They cheer when I hit the board at all, and I can't help but laugh along with them.

It feels good to let loose, to stop thinking about the project or my dad or Claire. For a few hours, I'm just Malcolm, another guy at the bar, laughing at stupid jokes and throwing darts like an idiot.

The night stretches on, and the bar grows louder, the hum of conversation blending with the clink of glasses and the occasional burst of laughter from a nearby table. Someone orders another round, and the waitress barely pauses to ask if we need it before setting the tray down. I nurse a whiskey this time—Jason's recommendation. It's smoother than the beer, warming my chest without the bitterness.

"So, Reed," Jason starts, leaning back in his chair like he's about to deliver some profound insight, "what's it like working on *The Monument?*"

I freeze for a split second, the rim of the glass pressed to my lips. I shouldn't be surprised—it's not exactly a secret that I was plucked for the project. Everyone in the office knows, but they've always treated it like this untouchable subject, some forbidden thing they're not allowed to pry into.

"It's… a lot," I say, carefully vague.

"A lot of pressure, huh?" someone else chimes in. Olivia, I think. She's in charge of environmental compliance or something equally dull, and I've probably exchanged all of five words with her since she started.

"Sure," I say, shrugging. "But it's different. Better than punching out another version of Template B-244. Better than having to suck up to David." I chuckle.

Jason whistles. "Man, I'd kill for a shot like that. Unlimited budget, no guidelines… You're living the dream, Reed."

I force a smile. "Yeah. Something like that."

The table buzzes with excitement, everyone chiming in with their theories about the project. What it'll look like, where it'll go, whether it'll actually be the *last* monument or just another symbol of humanity's pride.

I should feel proud, listening to them talk about my work like it's some grand, mysterious thing. But instead, I feel the weight of their expectations pressing down on me, suffocating me in a way I didn't expect.

"It must be lonely, though," Olivia says, cutting through the noise. "Working on something that big, with no one else really… in it with you."

Her words hit harder than they should. I think of Claire, of the way we haven't spoken since that night in my apartment. Of the silence between us, the way it's grown heavier with each passing day.

"It has its moments," I admit, swirling the whiskey in my glass.

Jason claps me on the shoulder. "Well, that's what nights like this are for, right? Blow off some steam, forget about work for a while."

"Right," I say, but my voice doesn't carry the conviction I want it to.

The truth is, I don't know how to forget. Not about the project, or my dad, or Claire. The Monument feels like it's carved into my very being, and no matter how many drinks I have, no matter how much I laugh, it's always there.

I excuse myself after a while, stepping out into the cool night air. The city hums an aching static around me. I lean against the brick wall of the bar, taking slow, measured breaths.

For all the noise inside, out here it's quiet. Too quiet.

I think about going back in, about joining the others for another round, another game, another attempt to feel normal. But instead, I pull out my phone and scroll through my contacts, stopping on Claire's name.

I don't call. I don't text. I just stand there, staring at her name, as the city moves on without me.

I tuck my phone back into my pocket and stare at the streetlights across the road. Their halos blur slightly, and I realize I've had more to drink than I thought. The door behind me opens, spilling laughter and muffled music onto the sidewalk. Jason steps out, a cigarette is dangling from his lips.

"Reed," he says, spotting me. "Thought you Irish-goodbyed us for a second there." He lights the cigarette, the end glowing orange as he inhales. "Everything good?"

I nod, even though the answer feels complicated. "Yeah, just needed some air."

Jason leans against the wall beside me, exhaling a thin stream of smoke. "Can't blame you. Place gets loud as hell."

We stand in silence for a moment, the city stretching out before us. The contrast between the vibrant nightlife and the quiet moments like this feels strange—like the world is trying to remind me of its different speeds, none of which seem to match my own lately.

"You know," Jason says after a while, "I was actually surprised you came out tonight. You're not really… one of us, if that makes sense."

I glance at him, not sure whether to be offended or agree with him. "One of you?"

He shrugs. "Office drones. The people who keep things moving but don't ever do anything special."

"You're not giving yourself enough credit," I say, though I'm not sure I mean it.

Jason snorts. "Come on, man. We all know what we are. Hell, I knew the moment I took this job that I wasn't going to change the world. But you?" He gestures with his cigarette. "You've got that shot. The big one. And it's kind of amazing to see you actually take it."

I don't respond right away. His words should feel like a compliment, but instead, they twist in my stomach. Because as much as I want to believe I'm "taking my shot," the truth is I've been running on autopilot for weeks now. The Monument might be my design, but it's started to feel like it's controlling me, not the other way around.

"I guess," I finally say.

Jason studies me for a moment, then drops the cigarette and grinds it under his heel. "Well, just don't let it eat you alive, yeah? A lot of people are rooting for you, whether you know it or not."

I give him a weak smile. "I'll keep that in mind."

He claps me on the shoulder and heads back inside, leaving me alone with my thoughts.

For a moment, I consider leaving altogether—going home, pretending this night didn't happen. But instead, I push the door open and step back into the bar.

The noise hits me like a wave, and I spot the group still at our table, laughing and gesturing over another round of drinks. I slide back into my seat, and Olivia immediately passes me another beer.

"Thought you ditched us," she says, grinning.

"Not yet," I reply, raising the glass to my lips. It doesn't taste as bad as I remember.

As the night drags on, I try to let myself get swept up in their energy. I laugh at their stories, nod along to their jokes, even throw in a few of my own.

The night grows quieter as I step out of the bar for the final time, my coworkers still laughing and lingering inside. The city feels alive in a way that's hard to explain—muted, yet vibrant. The streets hum softly under the pale glow of streetlights, and the distant sound of a car passing through a puddle cuts through the still air.

I walk without purpose, the buzz of alcohol still warm in my chest, my thoughts looser than usual. It's not unpleasant, though my mind drifts in directions I didn't expect. Jason's words linger. *You've got that shot.*

I think about how close I am to finishing the Monument. It's getting there—months of obsessing over every line, every curve, every shadow it will cast when the sun hits it just right. And yet, standing here now, I wonder if it's becoming more of a weight than a triumph. I'm not close to done with it at all.

The ideas are perfect, yes. The execution will be flawless, sure. But somewhere along the way, it stopped feeling like mine.

I cross the street, my footsteps echoing faintly. My thoughts pull me back to Claire, even though I try not to let them. It's been weeks since we talked, and the silence between us feels heavier than it should.

I glance down a side street and realize it leads to her building. I stop in my tracks, staring at the lit windows in the distance. I've driven her home a dozen times, but I can't recall ever being inside her apartment.

Not tonight. I keep walking, the cool spring air sharpening my senses as I move toward home.

By the time I get back, the buzz is wearing off. I pour myself a glass of water, standing at the counter with the kitchen light casting faint shadows on the wall. The emptiness of the apartment hits me harder than usual.

As I turn to go to bed, my phone buzzes on the table. I pick it up, expecting a text from Jason or maybe Olivia, but the notification is from Claire.

The message is short.

"we should talk"

I stare at the screen for a long time, debating how to respond—or whether to respond at all. Finally, I set the phone down, letting the message sit unanswered for now.

I move to the window, looking out over the city. I think of the cherry blossoms in the park on the way to work. How they have opened, tiny bursts of pink scattered among the gray. Like the flowers, I feel fragile, unsure if I'll bloom fully—or fall apart.

May

The first day of May it rained—soft and unassumingly. A mist lingers in the mornings and makes the air smell fresh like the world is still waking up. Morning dew sits on the grass and makes it glisten.

Claire hasn't left my head.

I've been staring at her "we should talk" message for over a week, composing responses in my head but never sending them. Every time I picked up my phone, words tangled together—apologies, explanations, questions I wasn't ready to ask. Every time I pass her floor on my way to my office, I feel a tightness in my chest. But I couldn't bring myself to reach out. Maybe I was afraid of what I'd say—or what she wouldn't.

It's on a morning like this, one where the gray sky feels lighter than usual, that I finally see her again. I'm getting ready to leave my apartment, papers tucked under my arm, heading to grab coffee before another long day. The moment I step outside of my door, she's there, leaning against the wall, looking like she was ready to knock on the door.

I stop, caught completely off guard. She's wearing a summer dress that seems to absorb all the color in the gray hallway, leaving me momentarily breathless.

Her hair is different—shorter, with subtle waves that catch

the light. She looks beautiful in a way that I don't think I've ever seen. She looks like she belongs in a book in my dad's library. She looks up, and for a second, neither of us says anything.

"Hey," she finally says, her voice softer than I remember.

"Hey," I reply, my throat dry.

"I, uh…," she says, pushing herself off the wall. She hesitates, her eyes meeting mine. "Look, Malcolm, I just wanted to say I'm sorry. For how I acted. I shouldn't have—"

"No," I cut her off, shaking my head. "It wasn't just you. I wasn't in the right headspace, and I—"

"Shut up," she interrupts, holding up a hand. "Let me finish." She takes a breath, her voice steady now. "I was selfish. I came to your place thinking I knew what you needed, and I didn't bother to think about what you were going through. That wasn't fair to you."

For a moment, I don't know what to say.

"It's okay," I manage. "I think… I needed time to figure some things out. But I missed you, Claire."

The confession feels raw, unfiltered, and for a second, I wonder if I said too much. But then she smiles—small, hesitant, but real.

"I missed you, too," she says simply, before I can speak. "I missed your stupid face. Your obsession with the dumb tree in your office. The way you see the world like it's still worth saving. I missed getting coffee with you."

I open the door wider and step aside to let her in. She glances around my apartment, her eyes landing on the counter where the bottle of wine still sits, then the scattered sketches hung up on my wall. She gravitates toward the window, where you can see the park and the cherry blossoms that have given way to fresh green leaves. The city stretches out below us, a perfect grid of compliance and conformity. But Claire stands there like a deliberate error in the pattern, a curved line in a world of right angles.

We stand there for a moment, the world around us fading into the background. The rain has stopped.

And then she's in my arms. She laughs, really laughs, and it's like the colors I've been missing finally burst into my world again. She looks up at me and her face shows an unrelenting joy.

We decide to be late for work.

Her lips find mine with an urgency that makes me forget everything,

"I tried to stay away, I tried to take things slow with you," she whispers against my neck. "I tried to be professional, distant." Her fingers trace patterns on my skin that would never pass inspection. "But I think I just love you too damn much."

Her skin is warm beneath my hands, her body alive with a kind of symmetry that nature perfected long before humans tried to regulate it. I trace the curve of her spine.

Reality crashes back. My phone rings. Soon after, Claire's iPhone is ringing too. I get up and scramble to find it tossed on the floor. David. I pick up.

"An emergency meeting in the conference room?" I repeat on the phone. My face draws serious as I listen to him. It's a short call, on purpose I'm sure.

Claire fixes her hair while I put my shoes back on.

We are at the office in minutes. I walk in with Claire and head through the lobby. I take the elevator to the ninth floor, Claire doesn't get off at the seventh today. The elevator opens and the floor is empty. I head to the meeting room—it's crammed. Claire leans in the door frame.

"Effective immediately, all architectural education programs will be consolidated under the Standardization Authority. The position of 'architect' will be phased out in favor of 'compliance officers' and 'template administrators.' With that being said, there will be no new employees at Meridian Associates until further notice." David says without taking a breath. He pauses and lets his employees process the information before speaking again. "All junior-level associates, please see me in my office later." His voice sounds heavy but his tone is purely professional. He stands there without speaking as if to conclude the meeting. My coworkers stumble out of the tight meeting room one by one. I stay inside.

He sits back in his chair, a pensive look on his face now, like he's holding something back, like he's waiting for me to realize what's happening before he says it. He pushes a familiar gray folder across the desk. It's stamped with the Department of Architectural Standardization's seal. I take it, flipping it open to find memos from various firms. The tone of the words is clinical, devoid of any real heart. I scan through them, my stomach sinking lower with each passing word. My mind flashes to Professor Chen, who taught me to see beauty in precision. He's been fired, the memo says. The entire architecture department at Cooper Union, gone. Replaced by instructors specializing in standardization and compliance. Architecture is over. *Architects,* even. I don't speak. I look up at David and leave the room, taking the folder with me.

Jason catches me in the hallway after the meeting, his usual enthusiasm dampened. "What does it say" he asks, his voice low. "The folder. What does it say?" Olivia joins us, her face pale.

"They're saying the Monument will be the final original

design ever approved. After that, it's all templates. Forever." I say in a monotone voice. They stop walking as if expecting me to elaborate, but I don't.

I don't even look at them. I just can't be bothered right now. They're probably about to be fired anyway—or at least moved to a separate "Standardization and Compliance" sector.

The weight of it settles over me as I head back to my office. In the corner, the ficus tree stretches its leaves toward the light, growing in defiance of the system that surrounds it. I think of Claire, of the way her touch brought color back into my world. I haven't seen her since the meeting ended.

I find her in the archives during lunch, surrounded by stacks of old blueprints. These aren't the cold, computer-generated plans of today but hand-drawn masterpieces, full of flourishes and details that spoke to the soul of the buildings they represented. Soon, all of this will be digitized, stripped of its humanity, and destroyed.

"They can't erase all of it," Claire says fiercely, grabbing my hand. "They can't."

I stay with her for my lunch break and head back upstairs. The mood is grim.

I work on the Monument late into the night, an old habit that seems to be coming back. I pour everything I have into its design. The ficus tree in my office sprouts new leaves, even as others fall, adapting but never conforming. Claire brings me dinner, spreads blankets on the floor, and turns my sterile office into something warm and alive. I'm the last architect in operation. Nothing new after me.

Claire butts in, "You're not the last architect," she tells me while eating. "You're the first of something new."

But the pressure is crushing.

Every line I draw feels like it has to be perfect, like it has to say everything that will never be said again. I think about Professor Chen, about the students who will never learn to see the world the way he taught me to. I think about the history being erased, the creativity being smothered under layers of compliance and regulation. I think about Dad. What would he think about all of this?

The days go by and another memo arrives: "Final Architectural License Examination to be discontinued effective June 1st."

I should feel devastated, but I feel like this was predictable. The government turns us into their little cogs, making sure that everything looks awfully perfect. Glorified code enforcement.

I think about Claire. How she and I are building something together. Moments, memories, small acts of creative rebellion. Claire is my anchor.

David's words from the meeting haunt me. The announcement wasn't just a shift in policy; it was a death knell for everything I've built my career on. Yet here I am, pressing forward with what feels like the last gasp of originality.

It is almost June and May ends with one final memo. This one is different. It's not just an update—it's a directive. All existing architectural firms are to be restructured by the end of the year, their projects absorbed into the Standardization Authority. This memo wasn't sent via a gray folder, reprinted and put on everyone's desk. This memo was sent en mass via text. I read the words aloud to Claire that evening as we sat on my balcony, the city lights flickering like distant stars. She doesn't flinch.

They can take the title of architect, the freedom to design, the very essence of creativity. But they can't take the Monument.

And in some way I hate that. I hate that I'm immune to it all. I hate that I have to sit here and watch as my coworkers get molded into somebody who wears a gray suit and delivers Guidelines like Mr. Hammond.

This Monument will be my legacy. Not just for me, but for Claire, for my father, for Professor Chen, for the people involved in the Denver Incident, everyone.

June

The first week of June feels oddly peaceful, especially after everything that's happened. The sun filters through my office window with a steady warmth that makes the ficus tree thrive. Its new leaves stretch confidently toward the light, mirroring my progress. The Monument's design is picking up speed.

Claire brings me coffee in the mornings now, just like she used to, always a little too sweet, but I drink it anyway. Her laughter fills my studio when she sits on the edge of my desk, sketching her own designs while I fine-tune mine. My office like a safe haven for harboring her ideas. We've fallen into a rhythm, a quiet, unspoken understanding that feels like breathing. I never realized how much I needed her until now.

At Meridian Associates, things are… different. The junior-level employees are almost all gone. The ones who were permitted to stay were reinstated into "compliance officers." Whatever the hell that means. Their cubicle desks sit empty, stripped of personal touches—no family photos, no quirky mugs, no signs of life. Only the senior architects remain, their faces etched with exhaustion and quiet resignation. Which is normal, but it's heavier now. Meetings feel as though every word spoken is laced with tension. David doesn't even try to sugarcoat things anymore.

The office used to hum with a kind of chaotic energy—interns sprinting to meet deadlines, Jason cracking jokes at the water cooler. Now, it's eerily quiet, like the building itself is holding its breath.

Even Jason, who always seemed invincible, has started to falter. He stops by my office less often, his usual energy replaced with a tired smile. He's one of the officers now.

"Still working on the Monument?" he asks one afternoon, leaning against my doorframe.

"Yeah," I say, glancing at the latest render on my screen. "It's almost there I think. But, I've thought that before, so I really don't know, man."

He nods, his gaze distant. "It's going to be incredible. You're lucky, you know? To still have something to work for."

There's something in his tone that unsettles me—a kind of finality. But before I can respond, he straightens up and disappears down the hall.

Claire notices the shift, too. She doesn't say much about it, but I catch her looking at me with a kind of quiet determination, as if willing me to stay the course.

"Don't let them drag you down," she says one evening, sitting cross-legged on the office floor, surrounded by blueprints and takeout boxes. "You're doing something important, Malcolm. Don't forget that."

I don't. If anything, his words push me harder.

By the end of the week, I've made more progress on the Monument than I thought possible. The design feels almost like it's fighting back against the system that's trying to erase what it stands for. I feel a sense of hope, not for me or for Claire, but for the Monument's future.

But hope is a fragile thing.

By mid-June, the studio feels more like a sanctuary than a workspace. My office is cluttered with sketches, drafts, and tiny models of the Monument that Claire calls my "artifacts." The ficus tree has become a fixture in our routine—Claire waters it, talks to it like it's part of our team, and even joked about naming it.

"You're weird," I told her one evening as she tilted a mug of water over its base.

"You love it," she shot back, and she wasn't wrong.

But beyond the walls of my office, Meridian Associates is slipping further into an eerie sort of monotony. More than what it was. The absence of junior employees is glaring. The seniors, once vibrant with experience and stories to share, now seem to trudge through the days like ghosts. They were here when architecture was a form of art, but now it seems like they have forgotten, like they have graduated straight from a brand new "Guideline Compliance" course. I view them in the same ways I viewed the junior associates. It's like I'm the only one who sees it. Jason's jokes have dried up completely, replaced by a distant politeness that feels foreign. Olivia's desk has been emptied. Even David, who's always been the steadiest presence in the firm, seems unsettled. He walks through the halls with a clipped pace, his shoulders tighter than usual. There's a tension in the air that no one dares address, like we're all waiting for something to break.

One morning, I catch Claire staring at the empty desks across the floor.

"What are you doing up here? Your lunch break is at 11:00." I ask.

"Doesn't it feel wrong?" She murmurs, ignoring my question.

"All of it," she continues, gesturing vaguely to the office

around us. "This place used to feel alive. Now it's like a factory. Or, maybe more like a museum exhibit of what this place used to be."

I don't have an answer for her. Instead, I just nod and head back to my office. I agree with her whole-heartily.

She's been my anchor through all of this, her presence a constant reminder that not everything is falling apart. But sometimes I wonder if my anchor is properly set.

"You look like you've been thinking too hard," she teases as she walks in my office a little while later. She seems to have found something to get her mind off the empty offices. I think it was me.

"Occupational hazard," I reply, sitting down at my desk.

Claire leans over my shoulder, studying the latest rendering of the Monument.

"You're close," she says softly. "Don't drown in your thoughts again. I love you, Mal."

Her words light something in me—a spark of motivation that I desperately need. She always knows what to say and I love her for that. I give her a kiss and she leaves to head downstairs, back to the archives.

But, as the week goes on, whispers start circulating about another restructuring. Meetings are being scheduled with little warning, and the Department of Architectural Standardization has been unusually active, they've started sending memo after memo again, these ones with vague yet foreboding language.

It's been six months since they first assigned me the Monument, six months since I was chosen for this "special project." It's hard to imagine now, but back then, their words felt like a promise. They wanted someone who doesn't follow the rules. Someone who sees the world differently. That somebody was me.

Sitting in my office, I can feel the weight of their expectations like a storm on the horizon. Suddenly, my door opens, and in they walk—only two men and a woman this time, all dressed in gray suits that feel too stiff for the room. Their polished shoes click sharply against the hardwood floor, each step methodical, as if they're marking time.

I don't stand. They don't expect me to.

"Malcolm," the man in the center says, his voice low and controlled, "we've come to see how you were doing"

I nod, keeping quiet, keeping my gaze on the blueprints spread across my desk, though I can feel them circling me. Staring at me. Staring at my work. Yet, they always seem to have that air about them—like they're more interested in the person than the work itself.

"We're impressed by your dedication," the woman adds, her eyes scanning my office, landing on the ficus tree. It's grown over the past few months, its branches reaching up like it's trying to break free. "But we wanted to see if you're still on track."

I hold her gaze, feeling a flash of irritation. *On track? Of course I'm on track. This project has taken over my life. It almost cost me my fucking relationship with Claire. Hell, even the plant is giving me side-eye these days.* But I don't say anything.

"You're the one who chose me for this project," I finally reply, a hint of defiance in my tone. "I think I'm doing just fine."

The man smiles, the kind of uncanny smile that doesn't quite reach his eyes. "Of course, we know you're capable, Malcolm. We chose you for your creativity, your ability to think outside the box. You know, Malcolm," He takes a step forward, his gaze sharp. "We don't *trust* you, we trust the system that we've built.

Your vision *will* align with the bigger picture. This Monument *will* be the final statement. It's going to be the last piece of true design before everything is," he pauses, then continues, "before everything is standardized."

There it is again. *Standardized.* The word hangs in the air like a weight I can't shake.

"I've been working on it," I say, trying to keep my voice steady. "It's coming together nicely. On the track I'm working, I think it could just take a bit more time to finalize the details."

The woman steps closer, her heels clicking as she moves. "We understand. But you must understand that the world is changing, Malcolm. And the Monument must reflect that change, not resist it. We are not the bad guys."

I lock eyes with her, feeling the walls of my office close in. "I'm aware."

She holds my gaze for a moment longer, then turns to the others. They exchange quiet glances, and I can almost hear their thoughts—how they're trying to figure me out, test me.

"Tell us," the man in the center says, his voice turning more casual. "What's your vision for the Monument?"

I lean back in my chair, my fingers tracing the edge of the design. The sketches on my desk are almost done, but there's something in them that doesn't quite sit right with me. It's still too clean, too perfect. And yet, there's a beauty to it. A rebellion beneath the surface.

"I see it as a symbol of what we've lost," I say, my voice quiet but firm. "It's not just about the structure. It's about remembering what once was... I'm not just- *We're* not just building something to comply with the future. We're remembering the past in a way that no template can."

The woman raises an eyebrow. "That's a bold statement.

You're sure that's what you want to say with this? Because, Malcolm," Her voice softens, but not in a soothing way. She steps closer to me and bends down to be on eye level, "Once it's built, it's not just your message anymore. It will belong to everyone."

I nod slowly, I try to seem like I'm unbothered, like nothing they said unsettled me. "That's the point."

There's a brief silence as they take in my words, weighing them.

Finally, the man nods. "Thank you, Malcolm. We trust you're on the right path."

They turn to leave, their steps sounding heavier than when they arrived. The door shuts behind them, and the office feels eerily quiet once again. I sit there for a long time, staring at the plans in front of me, wondering if I've said too much. Too little? If I've pushed too far? I sit in the silence that follows their departure, the sound of my own breath filling the space. It's strange how quickly they can leave, how quickly the world shifts back into its usual hum. The tension that lingered with their presence seems to dissolve, leaving me with nothing but the weight of their words. *We trust you're on the right path... We are not the bad guys.*

I don't let myself linger on it for too long. Instead, I turn my focus back to the project. The Monument. The design. I run my hand over the blueprints again, trying to make sense of the creeping unease in my gut. I load up my CAD program and render the several different models I have created.

It's hard to pinpoint what's wrong. The lines are clean. The angles sharp.

My eyes drift to the ficus tree in the corner. Its leaves have grown fuller, more vibrant. In a way, it feels like my only ally in this sterile building, its organic form the only thing that defies the perfection around it. I step over to it, running my fingers over a leaf, feeling the texture. The tree doesn't bend to the rules. It just grows. I think about the trees in the park. I think about the damn ducks.

I wonder if I'm still capable of that. Of growing outside the lines.

The phone buzzes on my desk, pulling me out of my thoughts. It's Claire.

How's the project going?

I smile at her message. A reminder to me that this isn't everything. That there's more to life than just what's in these walls. I'm pathetic.

I type out a quick response, *It's going fine. Just a lot of pressure. The gray-suit losers came back.*

Before I can hit send, a follow-up message appears. *Want to get dinner later? At my place?*

I pause, my thumb hovering over the screen. The weight of the day, the pressure from the meeting, all of it feels lighter at the thought of seeing her. I know I need to get back to work, but part of me craves the simplicity of a quiet evening with her. The way we don't have to talk about all of this—about the Monument, about the future, about what's slipping away. We can just exist.

Please.

I put the phone down, trying to shake off the lingering thoughts of the meeting. The truth is, the more I think about it, the more I realize—this project isn't just about building a monument. It's about creating a legacy. But whose legacy?

David's? The Standardization Authority's?

Or mine?

I walk over to the window, looking out at the city. The buildings stretch out in every direction, perfect and uniform. A grid, neatly aligned. Everything is in its place. Everything is exactly as it should be.

Except for the one thing that still isn't. Me.

The phone buzzes again. It's Claire, asking if I want to pick up food or if she should.

I smile, my fingers tapping the keys. *I'll grab it. I'll meet you at your place?*

I hit send, knowing that tonight, for a few hours, I can leave this place behind. Let the pressure fade. Just for a little while.

And when I do come back to the office, I'll be ready. Ready to finish what I started. Ready to build something that no one else can take away from me.

Dinner with Claire is simple, but it's everything I need. We sit at her modest dining table in her small, dimly lit dining room, away from the sterile glow of the office. The conversation flows easily, just like it always has between us. We don't talk about the project. We don't talk about the Standardization Authority, or the meeting, or the pressure that's been building. We talk about everything else—memories from college, plans for the weekend, little moments that make the world feel like it's still turning in a way we can control.

Her laughter fills the space, making everything around us seem brighter, even as the world outside grows darker with the night. There's something comforting about being with her, like we're holding onto something real, something that doesn't need to fit the mold of perfection that the world demands.

I catch myself smiling more than I have in weeks, the weight of everything else easing off my shoulders with each word we share. I let myself forget. Forget the project. Forget the future.

Forget the looming expectations.

We finish our meal and I take myself to the kitchen. An unopened bottle of Prosecco. I pour her a glass, and pour myself an even larger one. The streets are quiet now, the hum of the city softer in the cool night air. I sit on the sofa with her and we look out the window. We don't speak much as we watch, but it's the kind of silence that feels comfortable. Like we don't need words to say what we already know.

"You know," she says, her voice quiet, "I've been thinking about what you said earlier. About how this project isn't just about the design. It's about the legacy."

I nod, unsure of what to say.

"I don't think it has to be just about what *they* want," she continues, her hand gently resting on my arm. "I think it can be about what you want, too. What you're leaving behind. The way you see things. The way you see *us*."

I glance at her, the words catching in my throat. I feel a spark of something real. Something that isn't clouded by the weight of responsibility or the pressure to conform.

She smiles, and for a moment, I feel like I'm seeing the world through a different lens—one that's not just defined by expectations, but by possibility.

"I think you're going to figure it out," she says softly. "Whatever it is, whatever comes next."

I scoot closer to her, wrapping my arms around her, still holding my liberating glass of wine. It's just her and me. Just us.

I can't help but feel a sense of peace as we stand there, wrapped in each other's arms. The world feels right, even if just for a moment. Without a word, she pulls me in, her lips finding mine again. The kiss is slow, lingering, like we're both letting go of the tension we've been holding onto for so long.

July

July's rain was relentless, drumming a steady rhythm against the concrete outside. The buildings towering over the streets, their edges blurred by the persistent drizzle. Inside, I sit hunched over my desk, the faint glow of the monitor illuminating my face.

I've been visiting the archives more and more recently. Not just for Claire, but to search for inspiration. Technically, it isn't allowed, but the archive's team is small and The Monument gives me a sort of authority to have access to restricted material. Or at least that's what David thinks.

The archives have become my sanctuary. Towering shelves of forgotten artistry overhead, filled with sketches, paintings, and models. Every time I step inside, I feel the quiet hum of history.

Claire had been helping me navigate the mess of forgotten treasures, guiding me to the pieces that were kept locked away in the higher stacks. She joked once about coming here to survive the apocalypse—the endless labyrinth of shelves would safeguard her. She'd roll her eyes and smirk when I handed her a list of the materials I wanted access to, then playfully reminded me that she could tell David that I don't actually have access to this stuff.

"This one," she'd said last night, setting a stack of brittle blueprints in front of me. "You might like it. It's a cathedral design from the early 1900s—never built, but its details are incredible."

She was right. The designs were intricate to the point of madness. Carvings of mythical creatures lined the columns, and the arches swirled into impossible patterns that seemed to defy gravity. I'd stayed in the archives for hours afterward, imagining how the structure would look if someone had dared to build it.

This morning, I find myself going back to those sketches. They sit sprawled across my desk now, alongside notes I've made for The Monument. I trace my fingers over the lines of the cathedral blueprints. The designs weren't practical. They didn't make sense by today's standards. But they felt alive.

Claire steps into my office with two mugs of coffee, interrupting my thoughts. Her hair is tied up, and there's a relaxed softness in her smile. She's beautiful; I feel giddy inside.

"You were up late," she says, setting one mug beside me.

"Caught me," I reply, leaning back in my chair. I smile at her.

She glances at the sketches, her lips curving into a faint smile. "Are these the ones I showed you?"

"They've been stuck in my head," I admit, gesturing to the pages. "There's something… fearless about them. Like the architect didn't care if it couldn't be built."

Claire sits down on the edge of my desk, her eyes scanning the room. It's a controlled chaos—half-finished sketches pinned to the walls, drafts of the Monument in various stages, and the ever-present ficus tree casting long shadows in the corner.

"Maybe that's the point," she says softly. "Not everything has to be realistic to be meaningful. You remember what they used to say, right? 'An architect's dream is an engineer's nightmare.' Or something like that."

I laugh. Her words settle into the air like the rain outside, steady and true. She reaches out, her hand brushing against mine. I hold it for a moment, letting the comfort of her presence remind me of what matters.

The room feels warmer with her in it.

"I should get back to work," she says, breaking the quiet. She leans down to kiss my cheek, her lips lingering just enough to leave me feeling rooted.

"Thanks for the coffee," I say, my voice lighter now.

As she leaves, I turn my attention back to my desk. The lines of the cathedral blueprint blur together with the ones I've been drafting for The Monument. There's a feeling building inside me, like I'm standing at the edge of something vast and unknowable.

I spent the morning sorting through dozens of files, cross-referencing designs that had been discarded decades ago. Some were revolutionary for their time, others crude sketches of ideas that never made it beyond the conceptual stage. It was inspiring, in a way, how these remnants of ambition persisted even after their creators were long gone.

Claire had left me alone earlier than usual to focus on her own projects, and the silence was deafening in her absence. The Monument consumed my thoughts, yet the more I worked, the harder it was to feel certain about anything. I'd added details here and there—minor flourishes that felt clever in the moment—but when I looked at the project as a whole, something still felt incomplete.

By mid-afternoon, I felt the strain creeping into my neck and shoulders. I stepped away from my desk, pacing slowly between the different sculptures and models I have in my studio. The faint smell of coffee lingered from the cup Claire had left behind, and the rain outside seemed to grow louder in the quiet.

For a while, I allowed myself to just exist in the space. No Monument, no expectations—just the muted light filtering through the rain and the steady beat of water against the glass. My mind wandered to my father, as it often did these days.

It had been a while since I'd seen him. Weeks? Months? Time blurred when I thought about it too hard. Mrs. Tran had sent me a few updates, though they'd grown less frequent. It wasn't neglect—I'd just convinced myself there was always time.

I was sitting back at my desk when the phone rang, the sound slicing through the air with sharp clarity. It felt out of place, too loud against the subtle backdrop of rain and my own quiet thoughts.

I glanced at the screen, my brow furrowing as I read the name. "Hello?"

"Malcolm, this is Mrs. Tran."

Her voice carried an unmistakable gravity, though it was softened by careful restraint.

"Mrs. Tran," I said, leaning forward. "Is my dad okay?"

There was a long pause, and I could almost hear her weighing her words.

"He's stable right now," she said at last. "But I think you should come by, Malcolm. Soon."

My pulse quickened.

"What's going on?"

"He's had a rough day. His vitals dropped earlier this morning—he's stabilized since, but..." She hesitated, her tone steady but tinged with quiet urgency. "I've seen this before. It might not mean anything, but it's better if you're here."

Her words settled into the room like a heavy fog.

"I'll be there," I said, already reaching for my jacket.

"Drive safe," she said softly before hanging up.

For a moment, I just stood there, my hand still gripping the phone. The world felt distant, muted. My father wasn't immortal, but the thought of him fading—really fading—was something I wasn't ready to confront.

The Monument loomed in the corner of my mind, a silent reminder of everything unfinished. I pushed the thought aside, grabbed my bag, and headed into the rain.

The standardized assisted living center looked exactly like every other one I'd ever seen when I was searching for one for Dad. Modular, clean, and utterly devoid of personality. Its design was functional to a fault—smooth, white walls with minimalist accents, fluorescent lighting that hummed softly, and identical chairs lining the hallways. If you'd told me it was a hospital or a high-end parking garage, I wouldn't have argued. I made my way onto the all familiar concrete porch.

My footsteps echoed as I walked through the entrance corridor, passing identical doors with small nameplates beside them. My dad's room was at the end of the hall past reception.

Mrs. Tran greeted me outside the room, her face lined with exhaustion but still managing a soft smile.

"He's awake," she said quietly. "But his breathing's… it's hard."

I nodded, my throat too tight to reply.

When I stepped inside, the first thing that struck me was how small he looked. My dad had always been a towering figure in my life, but the man in the bed now seemed shrunken, his frame swallowed by the crisp, white sheets. The oxygen mask covered most of his face, and the steady hiss of the machine filled the otherwise silent room.

"Hey, Dad," I said, forcing a smile as I moved closer.

His eyes opened slowly, and for a moment, there was a flicker of recognition.

"Malcolm," he rasped, his voice barely audible over the mask.

"Yeah, it's me." I sat down in the chair beside his bed, leaning forward so he wouldn't have to strain to see me.

He looked at me for a long time, his gaze heavy with something I couldn't quite place. Regret? Pride? Maybe both.

"You… working too much?" he asked, each word labored.

I let out a soft laugh, though it felt hollow. "Always. You know me."

A weak chuckle escaped him, but it dissolved into a fit of coughing that made me flinch. His chest heaved, the sound rattling and wet, and I reached out instinctively to steady him, though there was little I could do.

"Easy," I murmured. "Take it easy."

When the coughing subsided, he sank back into the pillows, his breathing shallow and uneven.

"They… tell you?" he asked after a moment.

I hesitated. "Mrs. Tran called me. She said it might be… *time*."

His eyes closed briefly, as if the confirmation brought both relief and dread. "Figures," he muttered.

For a while, neither of us spoke. I just sat there, listening to the faint hum of the oxygen machine and the rain outside.

"I'm sorry," he said suddenly, his voice cracking under the weight of the words.

"Dad—"

"No, let me…" He paused to catch his breath, his hand trembling as he reached for mine. "I should've been… better. For you. For your mom."

"You don't have to—"

"I do," he insisted, his grip tightening despite his frailty. "I didn't leave you much, Malcolm. Not money, not... guidance. Just my damn stubbornness."

I swallowed hard, my chest tightening. "That stubbornness got me here, Dad. It's not all bad."

His lips twitched into a faint smile, but it didn't reach his eyes.

"You're a good man," he said softly. "Better than I deserved."

I wanted to argue, to tell him that he'd been enough, that he hadn't failed me the way he seemed to believe. But the words caught in my throat, and all I could do was hold his hand and hope he understood.

The hours passed slowly as I sat with him, each breath he took a reminder of how fragile it all was. Mrs. Tran came in periodically to check his vitals, her presence a quiet reassurance in the background.

As night fell, the rain continued its relentless rhythm, and I stayed by his side, unwilling to leave.

The night deepened, but sleep never came. I continued by his side, my fingers brushing against his hand as if holding on would keep him here just a little longer.

Mrs. Tran had pulled up a chair in the corner, a book balanced on her lap though she never turned the page. She glanced at me occasionally, her eyes offering a quiet understanding that words never could.

"Malcolm," my dad whispered.

I leaned in, my heart pounding at the sound of my name. "I'm here."

He shifted his gaze to the window, his pale eyes cloudy but still holding that stubborn spark I'd always known. "Do you... remember the lake? It was around this time of the month...

Fourth of July… we watched the fireworks on the dock after a long day of fishing… I miss the fireworks."

"Of course, I remember," I said, a smile tugging at my lips despite the ache in my chest. "You used to make me carry all the fishing gear because you said it'd build character."

His laugh was barely a breath, but it was there. "It worked, didn't it?"

I nodded, swallowing hard. "Yeah, Dad. It did."

He closed his eyes, his chest rising and falling with a painful slowness. "You ever take her there?"

Her. Claire.

"No," I admitted. "But I should."

His lips quirked upward. "She's good for you. Don't let her go, okay?"

"I won't." The promise felt heavy, like a weight pressing against my ribs.

For a while, he didn't say anything. His breaths grew more uneven, the spaces between them stretching longer and longer.

"I wish I'd done more," he murmured again, his voice so faint I had to strain to hear it. "More for you and your mom."

"You did enough," I said firmly, leaning closer. "You gave me what you could. That's all anyone can do."

He opened his eyes again, and for a moment, the sharpness in them returned. "Make this monument yours, Malcolm."

"Of course," I said, my throat tightening.

"Good," he breathed, his hand relaxing in mine. "That's my boy."

And then it happened.

At first, I thought he'd simply drifted off to sleep. His chest rose, fell, and then… nothing.

The silence that followed was deafening. No labored breathing, no rasping coughs, just the faint hum of the oxygen machine and the distant patter of rain.

"Dad?" My voice cracked as I leaned closer, gripping his hand tighter. "Dad?"

Mrs. Tran was at my side in an instant, her hand on my shoulder. "Malcolm," she said softly, her tone steady but heavy with finality.

"No," I whispered, shaking my head as if denying it would change the reality unfolding in front of me.

She reached over to turn off the oxygen machine, the hiss cutting off abruptly. The room felt impossibly still, as if the air itself was holding its breath.

My dad's face was calm, more at peace than I'd seen him in years. The lines of pain that had etched themselves into his features were gone, replaced by something almost serene.

I stayed there for what felt like hours, my hand still wrapped around his, unwilling to let go.

Mrs. Tran stepped out quietly, giving me the space I didn't even know I needed. When she returned, she held a small, folded blanket and draped it gently over his body, her movements slow and deliberate.

"I'll handle everything," she said softly. "Take your time."

I nodded, unable to speak.

Eventually, I stood and walked to the window. The rain had stopped, leaving the city bathed in a soft, silver light. The buildings still towered over everything, unyielding and indifferent, but for the first time, they felt small.

I turned back to him, my chest tight with a mix of grief and gratitude. He was gone, but the weight of his words and the memories we shared lingered, grounding me in a way I hadn't expected.

I had to go eventually, as I left the room, I looked back one last time, the image of him resting peacefully burned into my mind. I didn't cry, not yet. There would be time for that later.

For now, all I felt was the enormity of the moment and the silent promise I'd made to him.

The drive home was a blur, the city lights smearing together like watercolors through the rain-streaked windshield. I didn't turn on the radio. The silence felt heavier than any music could, pressing down on me, wrapping around me like a second skin.

When I finally pulled up to my building, the weight of everything hit me all at once. My legs felt unsteady as I climbed the stairs, my hand gripping the railing like a lifeline. Inside, the studio was dark, save for the faint glow of the TV across the room.

Claire was waiting. She was perched on the edge of the couch, her knees pulled to her chest, the worry etched into her face deepening when she saw me.

"Malcolm," she said softly, standing as I closed the door behind me.

I didn't say anything, just dropped my bag and walked straight into her arms. She didn't ask questions, didn't try to fill the silence with empty words. Instead, she held me, her hands running gently along my back, grounding me in a way that nothing else could.

"He's gone," I said finally, the words catching in my throat.

She tightened her grip, her chin resting on my shoulder. "I'm so sorry," she whispered.

For a while, we just stood there, wrapped in the quiet comfort of each other. My thoughts raced, fragments of conversations and memories flashing through my mind like an old film reel. His laugh, his sharp wit, the way he'd always held onto that stubborn streak even when the world seemed determined to wear him down.

"I didn't say enough," I muttered, pulling back slightly to look at her.

She shook her head, her hands finding mine. "You were there. That's what matters."

I nodded, but the knot in my chest didn't loosen.

We sat on the couch, the rain picking up again outside. Claire leaned into me.

"I feel like I should be doing something," I said after a while.

"Like what?"

I hesitated, running a hand through my hair. "I don't know. Something to honor him, I guess. But everything feels... too small."

She didn't respond right away, letting the silence stretch. "It doesn't have to be big," she said eventually. "Sometimes the small things matter more. What did he care about most?"

I thought about that. The lake, the stories he used to tell, the quiet way he found joy in little victories. "Family," I said finally. "And being stubborn as hell."

Claire smiled faintly, her fingers brushing against mine. "Then start there. Keep him alive in the way you live, not in some... grand gesture."

The simplicity of her words hit me harder than I expected.

We stayed up late, talking in hushed tones, sharing memories of him, and eventually drifting into a comfortable silence.

When morning came, the rain had stopped all together, leaving the city bathed in a pale, golden light. It didn't feel like the start of something new, but it didn't feel like the end either.

It felt like a pause—like the world holding its breath, waiting for what would come next.

I sat in my apartment, the hum of the refrigerator filling the silence. The condolence messages on my phone already started to pile up like obligations I'm too exhausted to answer. I know I should cry, scream, or do something that feels human, but all I feel is the weight of it—heavy, suffocating, like the air itself is pressing down on my chest. My hand drifts instinctively toward the drawer where I keep the pills, fingers brushing the cold bottle. Just one. Just enough to dull the sharp edges, to turn this chaos into something manageable. But as I grip the bottle, I freeze.

I clench the bottle tighter, the temptation clawing at me. I know it's a lie—one pill won't bring shit. It'll only bury the grief. I set the bottle down, but I don't put it back in the drawer.

The days after that blurred together. I remember sitting at my desk at work, staring at the dim screen, my thoughts spiraling like a storm. Every memory of him—the good, the bad, the messy—clashed with the weight of what came next. Cremation wasn't cheap, not even in a world where burials are practically myths.

My mind kept circling back to his final words. They rang in my ears like a challenge, like a curse.

I clenched my fists, leaning forward, my face inches from the monitor. If this monument was supposed to be my magnum opus, the culmination of everything that everybody ever stood for, then it needed to be more than just another structure. It had to be personal. His voice would be part of it. But first, I needed to lay him to rest—and I wasn't about to drain my savings for the privilege.

By the time the idea formed, it felt less like a thought and more like an inevitability. The gray suits wanted rebellion? They wanted *me*? Fine. But they were going to pay for it—literally.

The Standardization Authority headquarters was an imposing structure, a massive block of reinforced concrete that stretched into the sky like a monolith. Everything about it screamed permanence and control, from the colorless façade to the absence of any identifying features.

I marched through the revolving doors, my steps echoing against the polished stone floors. The reception area was clinical, devoid of warmth, just rows of desks and suits bustling back and forth. A woman at the front desk glanced up from her screen.

"Name?"

"Malcolm Reed." My voice was sharp, clipped. "I'm here to speak with someone about The Monument."

Her eyebrows lifted slightly, but she didn't argue. Instead, she typed something into her console and motioned for me to wait.

It wasn't long before a man appeared. His suit was gray, like the others, but he wore it with a kind of authority that suggested he wasn't just another cog in the machine. His face was unreadable, his movements deliberate.

"Mr. Reed," he said, his tone neither welcoming nor dismissive. "Follow me."

We walked through endless corridors, each one identical to the last. When we reached a conference room, he gestured for me to enter. I did, my heart pounding, my anger sharpening my resolve.

The room was sterile, the air heavy with the faint hum of concealed machinery. Two more suits waited inside—a man and a woman, both with the same expressionless demeanor.

"Let's make this quick," I said, taking a seat without being asked. "I need funding."

The first man raised an eyebrow. "Funding?"

"For my father's cremation." I leaned forward, locking eyes with him. "It's only fair. You've demanded everything from me for this project—my time, my creativity, my life. Now, I'm demanding something from you."

The woman folded her hands on the table, her face impassive. "Mr. Reed, the Standardization Authority doesn't typically handle personal expenses."

"Then you can consider it a condition," I shot back. "No funding, no Monument. It's that simple."

Silence filled the room, thick and suffocating. The three of them exchanged glances, their expressions shifting ever so slightly.

"You're serious," the second man finally said, his tone laced with something that might've been disbelief or amusement.

"Dead serious," I said, my voice steady. "You wanted rebellion. You wanted someone who wouldn't adhere to your precious guidelines. Well, congratulations—you got me. Now, you can either meet this one demand, or you can find someone else to finish your precious fucking Monument."

The woman leaned back in her chair, her gaze piercing. "Do you understand what you're risking? This isn't just about you."

"Do *you* understand?" I countered. "This isn't just about a monument. It's about what it stands for. If I can't even honor my own *father*, then what's the point?"

Another tense silence followed. Finally, the first man sighed, leaning forward. "We'll approve it. Consider it… an advance. But understand, Mr. Reed, that this project is bigger than you, or your father, or anyone else. Don't lose sight of that."

I stood, my jaw tight. "Don't worry," I said, heading for the door. "I haven't."

As I stepped into the hallway, the weight on my chest felt slightly lighter, though the fire in my gut still burned. They could try to control the world, to stamp out individuality, to make everything *standardized*. But they couldn't anticipate me.

And they couldn't stop me from making it mean something.

I threw myself into the project after the meeting. Every brush-stroke, every pencil mark, every detail became an extension of the emotions that had been festering inside me since my father passed. Anger, grief, guilt—it was all there, captured in the design, in the work.

The studio, usually a place of meticulous planning and clear-headed decisions, had transformed. It was now a battleground. I tore through materials like they were the very fabric of my frustrations. There was no room for subtlety; no time to second-guess. If I was going to finish this, it had to be raw. It had to be real.

Claire noticed. Of course she did. She always did. But this time, there was a shift in her concern.

She came by the studio, the door creaking open with a quiet protest as she stepped inside. The faint hum of the lights above was the only sound, aside from the soft scratching of my pencil across the sketchpad.

"Mal," she started, her voice tentative, "you're pushing yourself too hard again."

I didn't look up from my work. "I'm fine."

"You're not fine," she replied softly, walking closer, her eyes scanning the chaos of papers and scattered tools. "You're putting everything into this, and I get it. But it's not good for you. You're still grieving, and this obsession with finishing—"

"I *have* to finish it," I cut her off, not wanting to hear what she was saying. "This is for him. I don't care if it's not healthy, or if it's too much. I'm doing it for my father."

Claire was quiet for a long moment. Her eyes searched mine, looking for the man she knew beneath the storm I was becoming.

"I know," she whispered finally, "but this just isn't how you heal. You're just burying everything in your work. You're not letting yourself feel it."

I could feel the weight of her words, but I couldn't let them in—not now. "I can feel later."

Her lips pressed together in a thin line, and she took a slow, measured step back. "I know you're doing this for him, Malcolm. But don't lose yourself in it."

"I won't." I finally looked up, meeting her eyes for the first time since she'd entered the room. "I won't lose myself. Not after last time."

She stayed quiet, her gaze lingering on me for a few more seconds before she finally nodded. But there was no comfort in the gesture, only concern.

"I'll be here," she said, her voice soft. "But you have to promise me you won't forget to breathe. And don't forget to water the damn plant!"

I didn't answer her, but I smiled. I return my gaze to the work in front of me, feeling the emotion pulse through my veins, drowning out everything else.

The next few weeks blurred into one another. Days melted into nights, the hours spent hunched over the desk turning into weeks, and still, the design was never finished. There was always something missing, some piece of my father's memory I couldn't quite capture. But I didn't stop. I couldn't. The pressure, the pain, the drive—it all fueled the Monument.

Claire didn't stop checking in. Every time she came by, I saw the same mixture of support and worry in her eyes. She was doing everything she could to be there for me, but I wasn't letting her in. Not completely. Not when I was so close to something—something that felt like it might be the only thing that could redeem me.

The rain had returned, a soft drizzle that barely made a sound, but it was enough to blanket the city in that familiar, dreary hush. The streets, slick with water, reflected the glow of streetlights, their form blurred by the mist.

I found myself back at the archives. It wasn't a conscious decision. I had been avoiding it for weeks, but today, it felt like the only place I could go. My mind, too tangled with the Monument and the weight of my father's passing, needed something familiar. Something that belonged to him.

The room was still vast, the shelves towering over me like silent witnesses to all the forgotten memories held within. The smell of dust and old paper was comforting in a way, but it was also suffocating. I walked through the aisles, my footsteps muffled by the worn carpet, until I reached the section where the old blueprints were kept.

I pulled out the folder I was all too familiar with, my hands shaking slightly. It was his library design—the one he had spent years perfecting, the one that had inspired so much of his work. The floor plans, the elevations, the sketches that captured his vision before the standardization swallowed it whole. The infamous spiral.

I opened the folder, the yellowing pages crackling under my fingertips. The library he'd always dreamed of, designed with the same care and thought he'd poured into everything else. The angles were precise, the structure solid. There was a beauty in the chaos of it, in the way it seemed to flow, like the building itself had a soul.

For a moment, I couldn't breathe. The weight of it hit me all over again, the finality of his absence, the realization that I would never get to walk through those halls with him. This was the last piece of him I had left.

I traced the lines of the blueprint with my finger, the curve of the walls, the way the light would spill through the windows at different times of day. I could almost hear him talking about it, explaining his choices, his vision for the space.

It wasn't fair. I had poured so much of myself into the Monument, tried so hard to finish it for him, but it would never be enough. It would never bring him back.

But as I stared at the design, something shifted. The anger that had consumed me for weeks, the grief that had threatened to swallow me whole—it all seemed to fade into the background. There was still a part of him here. In this design, in the details, in the way it felt like he was still reaching out from beyond the grave.

August

The studio was a mess. I'm a mess. The only thing that remained constant in this place was that plant in my corner. Everything else; paper, blueprints, and discarded tools were scattered across the floor, evidence of the late nights, the anger, the frustration. But it was nearly finished. The Monument was standing tall now, its structure coming to life in a way that felt almost impossible just a few months ago. I can only hope that this month goes by quicker.

It wasn't perfect. The edges weren't smooth, the lines didn't align the way they should. But there was something beautiful about its imperfections, something raw and real that the world hadn't seen in a long time, something that Dad would like. I stepped back, my hands covered in dust and paint, and took in the view. One side of it was a tower of raw, unfinished metal, twisted and contorted into an abstract form that mirrored chaos and control at once. The top was open, a jagged peak reaching into the sky, and beneath it, the structure curled inward like a wound still healing. It's so close, it's just... blurry.

I could almost hear my father's voice—telling me to keep going, telling me to finish it, no matter how it turned out. And for the first time since he died, I felt like I could.

But there was still one thing left to do.

I wiped my hands on my jeans, picked up my phone, and dialed the number I'd been avoiding for weeks. For years. It rang once, twice, then she picked up.

"Malcolm?"

"Mom," I said, my voice softer than I expected.

There was a pause on the other end. "How are you?"

I swallowed hard. "I'm… alright. I just—can I come by?"

"Of course."

I hung up, my heart heavy but not entirely with grief. It had been years since I'd seen her. After the divorce, after everything, we'd barely spoken. I knew I had to see her. It wasn't just for me. It was for him. She didn't show up at Dad's memorial service. I'm not mad at her, seeing her only son in shambles and not having anybody to lean on would have broken her. I'm sure that she could use my company, now.

The drive to her house that afternoon felt longer than it should've. It was strange to think that I used to know every turn, every crack in the pavement, and yet it all felt unfamiliar now. The streets, the houses, the way the rain began to fall again as I pulled into her driveway—it all seemed distant.

I knocked on the door, my knuckles tapping lightly against the wood, and when she opened it, I saw her face for the first time in months. She hadn't changed much. Still the same, tired eyes, the same way her hair fell to the side, too much like mine. But there was a softness to her now, something that made me feel like I wasn't a stranger in her life.

"Malcolm," she said, her voice carrying that faint tremor. "Come in."

I stepped inside, and the silence that followed was almost too much. My mom had always been quieter than I remembered, though I couldn't tell if it was because of the years apart or the weight of what had happened. We stood there for a while, just looking at each other.

"I'm sorry about your dad," she said finally, and I could hear the sincerity, even if it had been buried under years of separation.

I nodded, swallowing the lump that threatened to rise in my throat. "Yeah. He… he didn't deserve it."

"He was a good man," she said, her voice thickening. "I know we didn't… always get along, but he was a good man, Malcolm."

"I know," I muttered, the words somehow feeling heavy, like I wasn't sure I should believe them anymore.

She gestured to the living room, her hands shaking as she moved to sit on the couch. I followed her, sinking into the cushions beside her.

"Are you okay?" she asked.

I thought about it for a moment, considering everything that had been happening—the Monument, the struggle, the anger, the need to make it all mean something. The grief that twisted and knotted inside me and wouldn't let go.

"No," I said quietly, "but I will be."

I didn't say much after that, just let the room fall into that familiar silence. It wasn't comfortable, but it wasn't as suffocating as I thought it would be. My mom sat across from me, fiddling with the hem of her sweater, avoiding my gaze. She always did that when we were younger—avoiding the hard conversations.

"You're working on something, aren't you?" she said after a while, her voice softer than usual.

I glanced at her, not sure how to answer. The Monument, the project that had taken on more weight than anything else in my life, had become an obsession. But I wasn't about to tell her that.

"Yeah," I said, keeping it vague. "Trying to finish it up."

"I don't want to pry," she added quickly, as if she knew I'd shut her out if she did. "But… I hope you're doing it for the right reasons, Malcolm. Not just for him."

I stiffened, surprised by her words.

"Doing it for the right reasons?" I echoed, feeling my jaw tighten. I wasn't sure where this was going, but I could feel the tension already.

She looked at me then, really looked at me, and I could see that she was struggling to put it into words, something between regret and concern. "You're not… trying to prove something to him, are you? Or to make up for what's missing?"

I opened my mouth, ready to snap back at her, but I stopped myself. She was trying to say something, something I wasn't sure I could hear.

"No," I said finally, my voice flat. "It's not like that. I just—" I broke off, unsure how to explain it. It wasn't just for my dad. It wasn't just for me either. It was something else entirely. Some invisible force driving me to create—to make sure the past was never forgotten, no matter how much the world changed. But it felt too hard to admit, even to her.

She nodded, her gaze drifting to the window. "I don't know what you're trying to do with all of this. But just remember, you don't have to carry everything alone, Malcolm."

I met her eyes, holding the silence a moment longer than I expected. It wasn't the kind of conversation I was used to having with her. And for once, I didn't feel like I needed to escape from it.

"I know," I said, then, for the first time in a long time, I let out a breath I didn't realize I was holding. "I know."

I stood up after a while, the conversation with my mom lingering in the background. It wasn't a resolution, but it felt like a shift. A small one, but it was something. I didn't know how much of what I was doing was for me, for my dad, or just to prove I could finish something that mattered. But the Monument—this thing I had poured every ounce of anger and grief into—was almost done.

The last touches were waiting for me in the studio. I could feel the weight of it in the back of my mind as I said goodbye to my mom, who was already pulling the worn-out coffee cup from the table, retreating into her own world again, whatever it was.

I had an idea of what the Monument was supposed to look like. The materials I chose were supposed to give it life, some sort of vibrancy that would represent everything I had been trying to channel into it. The base was a solid block of steel, unyielding, yet it flowed into the arches and curves that gave it shape, resembling the human form in its vulnerability and strength. Above it, an intricate network of glass and metal stood—twisting, like a giant ribcage almost, open and raw. It was abstract, yes, but everything about it felt personal, as though it had been forged by the same fires that burned inside me now. The work was too much—too intense—but in that intensity, I could see my father, see everything he had tried to teach me, in the folds of the design.

The sculpted metalwork reflected the sense of fractured memories I had of him. The imperfect shape, the asymmetry— it was what made it more real, more raw. But the centerpiece, the final element, was the glass at its core—a sheet of glass etched with symbols. An homage to his library's skylight detail.

I stood in front of it, letting the lines and edges settle in front of my eyes.

But the question remained: was it enough? Was it the right way to memorialize him? Or was it just a desperate attempt to make something last when everything was slipping away?

I pushed the doubt out of my mind as I pulled the final piece of glass into place. It clicked with a satisfying precision, and I stepped back, surveying the work from a distance. The Monument stood tall, shimmering with a quiet intensity.

I wasn't sure it was everything I wanted it to be, but it was the best I could give. And maybe that was enough.

But then, I think about what Mom said, about carrying my burden alone.

I felt the weight in my chest shift, just slightly, as if the air had thickened a bit. Maybe she was right. Maybe this was about more than just me carrying all of this alone, but in my gut, I knew I was the only one who could finish it.

As I closed the door behind me, the sound of rain still hammering against the windows, I felt a strange sense of finality. This project—this monument—had become more than just an assignment. It had become my way of grieving, my way of pushing forward when I wasn't sure what came next.

I couldn't bring my father back. But I could leave something for him in the only way I knew how: by making something that could stand, that could endure. Even if only for a while.

I stared at the Monument, unsure of how much longer I could keep standing there, questioning it. There was too much emotion wrapped up in every inch of it, too many expectations. It had started as something concrete, something I could control, but it kept shifting. I couldn't grasp it the way I thought I could.

My hands were still trembling slightly as I touched the edges of the glass. A part of me wanted to leave it. Walk away. But another part of me, the one I didn't fully understand, told me to keep pushing, to keep chiseling away at this thing until it made sense.

Then I heard the phone ring.

I had forgotten my phone was still on the workbench, buried beneath papers and tools. I picked it up without looking at the screen, and before I could say anything, the voice on the other end made my chest tighten.

"Malcolm?" Claire's voice came through, crisp but soft, like she was trying to read the room without seeing it.

I leaned against the workbench, staring at the Monument. I wasn't even sure if it was done, but I was still putting my hands on it, still working it like I could sculpt some kind of meaning into it, something real.

"Hey." I kept it simple.

There was a beat of silence on the other end, and I imagined her pacing, the way she always did when she was trying to figure out how to say something without making it sound like a question.

"You've been quiet lately," she said, not accusing, just stating it.

I shrugged, even though she couldn't see me. "Been busy."

Another pause, a little longer this time. "I know. I... just wanted to check in. See how you're doing."

Her voice was soft, warm, but there was something in it, something that kept me from brushing it off. It was just... her. It made me feel like I wasn't alone in all of this, even if the rest of the world felt like it was spinning in circles.

I took a breath. "I'm good. I mean... I'm figuring it out, I guess."

There was a quiet sigh, but she didn't push. "I'm glad."

It wasn't much, but it was all she needed to say. I could feel it—no demands, no expectations. Just… space.

"I, uh…" I looked at the Monument again, the steel and glass staring back at me, unfinished, like I was. "I've been thinking about the library a lot. Dad's library. It's… it's like I'm putting it all into this. You know?"

I could hear her smile. "I know."

I let the silence fill the room for a moment, feeling a weight shift, like I didn't have to carry all of this alone anymore. The anger, the grief—it wasn't gone, but at least now it had a place to rest.

"I should let you get back to it," she said, but there was an unspoken invitation hanging in the words. The option to reach out again, whenever I needed.

"Yeah," I muttered, a little more than I wanted to admit. "I'll see you soon, alright?"

"I love you." She paused again, like she wanted to say something else, but didn't.

The phone call drifted into silence until she said goodbye.

We both hung up at the same time.

There was a reason I kept pushing forward like this, alone, without asking for help. Because if I stopped, if I even paused, I was afraid I'd collapse into the pile of broken pieces I felt like I was becoming.

I stood and stared at the Monument in front of me, the glass reflecting the dim light. My father's absence seemed so final now, like I had spent so much time trying to carve something out of all that pain that I couldn't see anything beyond it anymore. The rest of the world felt distant, like I was watching it happen from the wrong side of a window.

And I just kept standing there.

Waiting for something to make sense. Then it did. The visions in my mind all clicked together.

September

September's morning light stretched long across the studio, filtering through the high windows in fractured slants. I sit at my desk, hands folded, staring at the final renderings of the Monument. Every line, every curve, every deliberate void stared back at me. The final piece of the computer render slid into place with a dull click of my mouse. I exhaled, stepping back, my eyes tracing over the Monument as if seeing it for the first time. It was done. Or at least, as finished as something like this could ever be. I was certain if given another month, another year, another decade, I'd still find things to tweak, angles to adjust, meanings to refine. But this was it. The scale model I had in my office looked down on me. I feel like I can see clearly now, the vision in my head like an extension of my own eyesight.

The studio lights cast sharp shadows across the surfaces, accentuating the contradictions I'd spent months embedding in the design—chaos within symmetry, organic forms and corridors within the monuments encased in a rigid structure, imperfections in a sea of precision. It was everything they had wanted, and yet, it was still mine, it was still the People's. I had made sure of that.

Claire was sitting on the old drafting table, legs swinging

slightly, scrolling through something on her phone. She had been there for hours, waiting, watching, occasionally offering commentary that ranged from insightful to insufferable. She eventually got up to water our ficus tree. I need to prune that damn thing one of these days. Not now, though. After.

"So, are you done staring at it, or do you want to make out with it first?" she asked, not looking up.

I huffed out a laugh, running a hand through my hair. "I should at least take it to dinner first."

"Bold of you to assume it's into you." She pocketed her phone and finally looked at me. "So? You satisfied?"

I want to say yes. I really did. But the word caught somewhere in my throat. I settled for, "It's done."

Claire studied me, tilting her head. "That's not an answer."

I sigh, rubbing my face. "It's as good as it's ever going to be."

She hopped off the table, stepping closer to stand beside me. "Which means it's perfect."

I let the silence settle, both of us staring at the thing that had consumed me for so long. Consumed our relationship.

"You know," Claire said after a moment, "I think people are gonna love it. Or hate it. Either way, you'll be responsible for some strong emotions. Which, really, is the goal, isn't it?"

I smirk. "That's the spirit."

Claire sat up and moved to the small sofa in my office-turned-studio behind me, lazily flicking through a magazine she had no real interest in. "So," she drawled, snapping the page closed with one hand, "you gonna tell me what the hell it actually is?"

I exhale through my nose, looking back up at it."It's not that simple."

"Oh, of course," Claire said, standing up and making a grand gesture. "It's never that simple. It's an exercise in liminality, an exploration of human perception, an introspective take on—"

"It's a monument, Claire."

She grinned, folding her arms. "And what's a monument, Mal?"

I dug myself into a whole here. There was no escaping this conversation. "It's built on contradiction," I started. "It's grand but empty. Recognizable but impossible to place. One side looks like a rising structure, the other like a collapsing one. The details shift depending on where you stand, like history."

Claire's expression softened just slightly. "So it's a mirror."

"Maybe. Or maybe it's just a shape we're all pretending means something." I stop and turn to Claire.

"Claire, this is it. I really think they'll like this. It's like… every dream I've had since this damn project started finally got put into the real world and they all morphed together, and-"

Claire cut me off with her elbow jabbing my ribs. "So, are we celebrating, or are we just gonna stand here contemplating your nerdy magnum opus?"

I looked at her, really looked at her, and I felt something other than exhaustion. I felt the opposite. I had forgotten about outside the city. Outside of the Monument and my office.

"Celebrating sounds good."

"Great. I'll get the drinks. You stare at it for five more minutes and say something dramatic to yourself."

And with that, she walked off, leaving me alone with the Monument. One last time. She seems so chipper. We hadn't talked much since last month after seeing my mom, but I think she is starting to realize that she's going to get *me* back. She's beaming, though. Practically bouncing on her heels, like she's been waiting for an excuse to act as if she owns the place. Which, to be fair, she basically does. The past few weeks have been a blur—finalizing the Monument, coordinating last-minute adjustments, fighting with engineers who don't understand why I need what I need. And now it's over. And Claire knows it, knows I've been running myself into the ground to make sure it's everything it's supposed to be.

She comes back in a few minutes later with some plastic cups and a cheap scotch. I take the cup from her, the weight of it grounding me in this moment, in this place. Claire taps hers against mine, her eyes sparkling in that way she gets when she's not holding back.

"Here's to the chaos we've both survived," she says, and I can hear the smile in her voice.

I drink. The burn of the scotch clears something in me. A fog, or maybe just the weight of all that had been building for so long. The weight of the Monument.

"So," Claire says, settling on the sofa, "you know what comes next, right?"

I hesitate, looking over at the piece, this twisted puzzle of a thing that now defined my entire life. "What do you mean?"

She leans back, taking a sip of her drink, watching me carefully. "The unveiling, the fallout... all of it. You're gonna have to answer for this eventually" Her fingers tap the side of her cup absently.

"I don't care," I say. "I've already made it. Everything else is... whatever."

Her eyes flicker, but she doesn't press. She takes another sip. She's right, of course. The fallout is coming, and I'd be lying if I said I didn't know it. I knew how people would react—hate it, love it, feel nothing at all, protest, make shirts about it. But now it's done, and I don't have to worry about what's next. At least, not yet. I've done so much worrying recently.

After a few long moments, she stands up, her eyes narrowing. "You wanna go somewhere?"

"What do you mean?"

"A road trip, Mal. You need to get outta here. We can celebrate, see the country, see what's left of it. I'm serious. It can be your early birthday gift to me!"

I stare at her. Her birthday. Shit. "Just like that? I finish my life's work and we just get up and leave? There's *nothing* else you wanna do for your birthday?"

She shakes her head. "Nope! You deserve a break. We both do. You're done with the Monument, and this place isn't gonna give you the answers you're looking for." Her voice softens slightly. "And honestly? Neither will the next project. Or the one after that."

I know she's right. I've been tied up in this for so long that I've forgotten what it's like to feel something that isn't frustration or triumph. What it's like to just breathe without needing a next step. Maybe I could use a road trip. Maybe that's exactly what I need. To leave behind the concrete and the Monument and everything that's been clawing at me. To leave behind Dad's death.

I stand, setting my plastic cup down and walking to her. "Alright, let's do it."

She smiles a grin that's just a little too confident. "I thought you'd say that, but I didn't think it'd be that easy. You're such a pushover for me."

"Shut up."

I give her a quick kiss and wish her a proper 'Happy birthday!'

I close down the studio, shutting off the screens and letting the silence settle over the room. The finality of it all hangs in the air like a thick fog, but I push it aside. I grab my jacket from the back of my office chair and head for the door, Claire already waiting outside.

"You're really serious about this, huh?" I ask, stepping into the hallway.

Claire nods, bouncing on her heels as she pulls on a light sweater. "I don't know what you're waiting for. You've got the world in your pocket now, Mal. A little vacation isn't going to ruin your masterpiece."

I can't help but laugh, following her to the elevator. "You act like I've spent years dreaming of this."

The car ride to her place is quiet, but not uncomfortable. She's not pushing for conversation, which is somehow more reassuring than anything else right now. The hum of the engine is the only sound. I'm sure she is saving all of her thoughts for the trip. How lucky am I?

When we get to her apartment, Claire wastes no time. She leads me inside, tossing her bags on the bed and then rummaging through her closet. "Pack light," she calls from the bedroom.

I find myself in her kitchen, staring into the half-open fridge. There's a bottle of water and some fruit, nothing particularly exciting.

Claire reappears in the doorway, holding a few pairs of clothes. She throws a small duffel bag at me. "I said pack, lazy! I'm driving. Pack. Now." She yells.

I catch the bag in one hand, the idea of just packing up and going somewhere feels almost like I'm rebelling.

I throw a few shirts and a pair of jeans I had at her place into the bag, realizing for the first time in months that I don't have to think about the Monument's perfection. There's something oddly freeing about that.

She grabs her things, and then we're back in the car, heading toward the highway. "Where are we going first?" I ask, turning to Claire. She looks at me trying to contain her smile and doesn't answer.

I lean back in the seat, my eyes drifting between the passing landscape and Claire, who's focused on the road but clearly enjoying the quiet. Her fingers tap lightly on the wheel to the rhythm of the song playing softly on the radio. The New Jersey landscape is nothing like what it used to be, but just the act of driving through the city on the highway makes me think back to when I was a kid.

We drive in silence for a while, the sound of the tires on the pavement almost hypnotic.

"You think people are going to like it?" I ask suddenly, my mind wandering back to the Monument.

Claire takes a second to think, glancing at me with a small shrug. "I think the people need something to love right now. And I think that the Monument is supposed to provoke something. Make people think. So, yeah I would say so."

I consider that for a moment, trying to shake the unease that comes with the weight of it all. "I don't know. I feel like it's too… much. Maybe they'll just see a giant thing and think, 'That's it?'"

She snorts. "If they don't see the depth in it, that's their problem. Not yours."

The words hit harder than expected, making me pause and think. I love her.

The night stretches on, and we finally stop for gas at a small, rundown station in a small middle-of-nowhere town near Gettysburg. The moon casts long shadows across the empty pumps. It feels like the world is holding its breath, waiting for something to happen.

Claire steps out first, her shoes tapping on the pavement as she stretches her arms overhead. "You good?" she asks, looking back at me.

I nod, feeling the weight of everything start to slip away, replaced by something else I can't quite name. It feels like the start of something, even if I don't know what that something is yet.

"Yeah," I say, getting out of the car and walking over to join her. "I think I am."

We drive a few blocks down the street, eyes scanning for a place to stay. The motels here are small, tucked away behind overgrown hedges and half-visible from the road. We pull into one that has a faded sign hanging off the side, a single light above the door flickering like it's not sure whether it wants to be on or off.

The office is small, the window cracked open just a little, and the man behind the counter is an older guy with glasses that look too thick for his face. He looks up as we enter, nodding at us as if he's seen this all before. He doesn't ask any questions, just hands over a key to a room in the back, the kind of place where you can park right outside your door. A kind of place you'd never see, let alone be able to design in the city.

We're the only ones in the lot, and the low hum of the fluorescent lights outside the room is the only sound breaking the stillness of the night. Inside, the room is small and simple. The beds are covered in faded floral comforters, the carpet a little frayed at the edges. The air smells faintly of cleaning supplies and dust, but it's a comfort in its own right, a pause from everything else.

I sit on the bed for a minute, the weight of the day still pulling at me. Claire kicks off her shoes, stretches out on the other bed, and lets out a sigh. "This'll do," she says, her eyes closing as she sinks into the softness of the sheets.

There's no pressure here, no rush to get things done or figure out what's next. It's just the two of us. I lie down and don't even bother changing-or doing anything. Claire gets up to take her shirt off before heading to the stand—alone sink outside of the small bathroom. I watch her as my eyes drift closed.

I wake up to Claire's body against mine and the sunlight streaming through the Tuscan-style curtains. I kiss her as she wakes up. For a moment, I forget we're in a cheap-ass motel and I just see her.

We get up after a while and get ready before heading out to check out of our room.

The air smells faintly of dust and gasoline, a sharp contrast to the sharp tang of city streets. We park outside a diner with a flickering neon sign, the kind that looks like it hasn't been fixed in years.

Inside, the smell of frying eggs and sizzling bacon greets us before we even step through the door. The booth we slide into is worn in the best way possible, like it's been around long enough to have a personality of its own. The menu is old-school, laminated and curled at the edges, with prices that seem like a throwback to another time. The waitress is older, her hands steady as she sets down two mugs of coffee with the practiced ease of someone who's done this a thousand times.

"Y'all traveling?" she asks with a curiosity that feels familiar in a town like this.

"Yeah," I say, glancing out the window. The streets are quiet, but I can almost feel the weight of the place—a town that isn't looking for the next big thing, that doesn't have any big dreams for the future. It's just here, existing in its own way. And that's kind of nice.

Claire looks up. "Just passing through," she answers, her voice soft but strong.

The waitress nods, as if she's heard that answer more times than she can count, and walks away. We settle into the booth, both of us taking in the slow rhythm of the town. People come and go, but nothing here really changes. It's like the outside world forgot about this place, but I'm not sure it minds.

Claire leans back in her seat, resting her head against the booth, her eyes half-closed but content. The coffee is strong, bitter, just like the way people talk about things that really matter here—without pretense, just the truth, whatever that is.

"Think we'll come back here someday?" Claire asks, her voice lighter now, not filled with the exhaustion we both feel.

I glance around the diner, at the worn floors and the faded faces, and then back at Claire. "Maybe. If it doesn't change."

We eat a quick breakfast before heading out again. I made sure to tip the waitress.

The town is quiet, their storefronts weathered but standing, like they've been waiting for something that never came. The roads are cracked, the signs faded, the people moving in rhythms dictated more by habit than by any broader cultural mandate. It's like the vast stretch of land outside the big cities never quite caught up with the world that's constantly changing. The houses aren't sleek and uniform, the colors aren't curated, and the architecture doesn't follow any strict guidelines—it's just real. There's no pressure to conform to any idealized version of beauty or purpose. It's raw and unpolished in a way that feels nostalgic, like stepping into a space where the world kept turning, but nobody really noticed or cared enough to regulate it.

The Content Standardization Act was the government's answer to control the "chaos." As smaller cities grew and technology advanced, things started to spiral. Too many voices, too many perspectives, too much diversity in thought and culture, the powers that be decided. It was overwhelming, messy, and unsustainable. The Act was meant to create order where there was none, to simplify, streamline, and make everything uniform. From art, to literature, to fashion, it all had to fit within an approved framework—one that prioritized efficiency, uniformity, and predictability.

The law was passed under the guise of efficiency and modernization. It promised to eliminate waste, make spaces more functional, and help citizens feel connected to a broader, more cohesive national identity. But in reality, it stripped away individuality. Everything had to look the same, feel the same. Local culture? Discarded in favor of a national aesthetic, an unspoken rulebook that dictated everything from colors to proportions, from signage to materials. Even religion was disbanded in some areas, not by the government but by their own citizens. Something that once gave me guidance and answers to lean on. But now we're too smart for it, right? Or at least that's how they've sold it to us now. You get your answers from artificial intelligence, Google supercomputers, from science. Nobody needs to question anymore.

People were no longer able to express themselves through the things they built or the art they created—everything was about practicality. Cities, with their buzzing energy, adapted quickly. But the countryside? It resisted. It didn't change as rapidly or as aggressively, and in some places, it was like time had simply stopped. The Content Standardization Act never quite managed to reach here—at least, not in the same way. These areas became the forgotten places, left behind as the country's more progressive vision was enforced elsewhere.

But even with all the changes that have swept through the country, there's still something untouched, something real about the places that the new laws can't quite reach. They feel like a different world, almost as though you're visiting a time capsule, preserved in its imperfection.

The sun was just beginning to rise as we hit the road again, the car humming along the highway like it had a purpose, like it knew exactly where it was going. Claire was driving now, her hands steady on the wheel, and I could feel the warmth of the morning light spilling through the windshield. It was a soft contrast to the weight of everything that had led us here, and for a moment, it felt like I could breathe again. The Monument, the city, all of it, seemed a lifetime ago.

"So," Claire said, breaking the silence, "I've been thinking about what was said yesterday. About the Monument being a reflection of history. What happened to all the actual landmarks? All the stuff that was, you know, real history? Were they just wiped out by the Standardization Act?"

I didn't even have to think about it. "The old stuff, the landmarks—no one knows what to do with them anymore. They don't fit the new narrative. They're inconvenient, nostalgic in a way that's harder to sell. The city's a perfect example. Everything is about efficiency now, you know? History doesn't really fit into that."

Claire's fingers tapped lightly on the steering wheel as she processed it. "I get it, but it feels wrong. How can they just erase history? Isn't that... dangerous? Like, what happens to our stories?"

I sighed, my gaze drifted to the cars ahead. "The thing is, they're not erasing it entirely. They're just... rewriting it. Landmarks won't disappear, but they'll be redefined, reimagined. Preserved in a way that makes them more digestible, more palatable to the new model. They might turn into digital recreations or interactive exhibits, but the raw, unrefined versions? They won't survive. You're the archivist, don't they train you on this stuff?"

Claire spoke again, "Malcolm, I'm ninety-nine percent sure they tell every employee a different story."

"So, you think that's what's happening to everything now? To people, to culture? We're just being re-developed?" She asks, continuing the conversation.

I didn't answer immediately, letting the words sit between us, heavy and real. "Maybe. People like a cohesive story. They want something simple, something easy to follow. Look at AI. It's not just about monuments or art anymore. The Standardization Act? That was about creating a world where everything aligns. Where everything fits perfectly into a box. The AI, the algorithms that we use in the office for the templates—they process everything, give us answers. The narrative it builds is so easy to follow. No more uncertainty. No more contradictions. It's all... clean."

Claire's eyes flicked over to me, narrowing slightly. "Is that what you think it is? Just a clean narrative?"

I let out a breath, feeling the weight of it all. "No, it's not just about the efficiency anymore. It's about control."

There was a long pause after that, then I suddenly broke the silence.

"Shit," I muttered under my breath, suddenly jolted by the realization. I had forgotten to tell David I was going on vacation.

Not like it mattered, right? Ever since the Monument project started, David had been little more than a figurehead. The Standardization Authority had essentially run the show, and David, for all his titles, had no real authority over me anymore. Still, he was technically my boss, and I had made a habit of keeping him in the loop—mostly to avoid any unnecessary confrontations.

I fumbled for my phone, pulling it out of my pocket, and quickly shot off a message to David.

Malcolm: Just realized I didn't tell you—Claire and I are taking a short vacation. Be back in a few days.

I hit send, and then, without looking at the screen, leaned back into the seat, watching the landscape blur past us. The silence stretched, but only for a moment before my phone buzzed.

David: The Standardization Authority stopped by. They wanted to ask a few questions about the final renderings. I told them you were unavailable.

My fingers tightened around the phone as I read the message. Of course, they stopped by. Of course they did. The Authority couldn't let me have even a few days to breathe. I couldn't help but roll my eyes.

Malcolm: Figures. Did they say anything else?

I waited a beat before David replied.

David: Yep. They said you're in charge of the unveiling now. You'll need to coordinate with the contractors and engineers to finalize everything. They want something figured out by the end of next month.

I sat there for a moment, staring at the screen, the weight of the message sinking in. The Authority wasn't going to let me off the hook so easily. Not that I expected them to, but damn it,

I had hoped for a brief escape. It felt like everything I did had been for them, and now they were breathing down my neck even in the middle of nowhere.

I leaned back in my seat, tossing the phone onto the passenger side. "Guess it's never really over, huh?" I muttered, half to Claire and half to myself.

Claire glanced at me, sensing my frustration. "You okay?"

I let out a deep breath, trying to let go of the tension. "Yeah. Just… the usual shit with the Gray Suits. They went me to lead the unveiling, you were right."

"Maybe that's good, you know it better than any engineer who has worked on it, and you damn well know it better than the Authority. You'll do great, Mal."

I let her words sink into me, marinate.

"I think you should know where we are going by now." Claire says, bringing me back to the road trip.

"I have absolutely no idea."

"You didn't see the massive roadside sign we just passed, huh? We're going to Shenandoah, my parents used to take me here all the time as a kid, and.. I don't know I thought that it'd be good for you."

"Then, I guess we'll have to take our kids here, too, one day." I say back with a hidden smile on my face.

"Oh my gosh, did my very own Malcolm Reed just flirt with me? Maybe we should start going on more road trips." Claire teases back and I can't help but chuckle.

The drive through Shenandoah felt like an escape. The winding roads cut through endless forests, the kind of greenery I hadn't seen in ages—real, untouched, breathing life into the surroundings. The sky stretched wide, a canvas of soft blues and golds, like it hadn't been altered by anything. No standardization, no guidelines. Just raw beauty. We pulled off the main road and parked at an overlook, stepping out into the cool breeze that seemed to carry the scent of pine and earth. The mountains rolled out before us, layers of green that softened the harsh edges of the world I'd been caught in for so long. Claire stood next to me, her eyes scanning the landscape, her body relaxed in a way that felt so foreign to me now. I hadn't realized how much I'd needed this—this quiet, this simplicity.

She turned toward me then, her face softer than it had been in a while. There was a tenderness in her gaze, something familiar, yet different.

She took a step closer, her lips curving into a slight smile.

I felt the tension in me slowly unwind as I met her eyes, her words settling in the quiet space between us. Everything had been so chaotic, so demanding. But in this moment, with her standing there, it felt like there was room for something else.

Before I could say anything else, she was close, her lips meeting mine in a kiss that felt like the answer to all the questions I hadn't known how to ask. In a few weeks, I would be standing in front of a crowd of hundreds, maybe more. But right now, the only thing that mattered was the girl in my arms.

October

Just a couple weeks into October came the morning of the unveiling, the air was thick with anticipation. The Monument has been installed and stands full-scale. It loomed just beyond the edge of the stage, an imposing yet elegant figure in the distance. There were last-minute touches, of course—adjustments to lighting, the placement of cameras, the occasional re-positioning of something to ensure the perfect shot. I was supposed to be in charge of it all.

But today, it wasn't the project itself that was consuming my mind; it was the speech I had to give. It wasn't something I'd thought about until now, and the weight of it was finally sinking in. A part of me had hoped someone else would take the reins—maybe David, or the engineers. But no, this was my moment. My responsibility.

A few of the key engineers were gathered around a large table in a small conference room on site. They looked just as uncomfortable as I felt. No one ever talked about this part of the process—the words. We'd built the Monument together, sure, but none of us had signed up to stand in front of a crowd and explain why it was important.

I stood at the front, fiddling with my notes, staring down at the blank page in front of me. Claire had told me to "wing it," but I wasn't sure how much "winging" would be allowed in front of a crowd this big, with the Standardization Authority watching closely.

"Well, we can't just start with 'Thank you, thank you, now behold,'" one of the engineers, Sam, said, shifting uncomfortably in his seat. "We need something… weighty. You know, something that lets people know that this wasn't just another project."

"Exactly," I said, tapping the pen against the paper. "We need to make it feel like it's about more than just stone and metal. This is about something bigger."

Claire, who'd slipped into the room quietly, leaned over my shoulder. "What about something personal?" she suggested, her voice calm but sure. "You built this. It's your legacy. Show them that. Talk about the process, the struggle, what it meant to you. Maybe talk about your dad."

"Struggle?" I muttered under my breath. "That's one way to put it."

"You're the one giving the speech, Malcolm," she teased. "You can frame it however you want." She gave me a quick kiss on the cheek.

I sighed, still looking at the blank page. I hated this part—the words never seemed to do the vision justice, and I was too tired to pretend otherwise. But then I thought about what Claire said. The struggle. The battles fought, the sleepless nights. It wasn't just a building—it was everything I'd been through.

"Okay, okay," I said, standing up straighter, my mind starting to sharpen. "I'll open with something personal. Something raw."

"That's the spirit," Claire said, smiling. "Now get to it."

I walked to the front of the room and began scribbling,

speaking aloud as the thoughts came together.

"This is not just a Monument; it's a reflection of everything that we are and everything we could be," I muttered, more to myself than to the group. "It's built on contradictions, on chaos and structure. On history and uncertainty. It's not perfect, and it never will be—but it's ours. It's a symbol of what we've built together, and what we can keep building, even when it feels like we're being pushed to the edge."

I paused, watching the engineers around me. They were listening now. Maybe I could do this. Maybe we could do this.

Claire stepped up behind me, placing a hand on my shoulder. "That's good, babe," she said, her voice full of conviction.

I nodded, feeling a little less like I was about to crack under pressure.

"Alright," I said, looking up at the group. "We've got a Monument to unveil."

The air carried a cool mist, now. Standing before my creation, anticipation was the only thing that consumed me. I had poured my soul into every curve and angle, each line a reflection of the journey that had led me here. Every feature of the Monument was a statement of rebellion—the soaring arches whispered of freedom, intricate carvings spoke to the vibrancy of human expression.

I glanced over the crowd before me, faces glowing with awe and expectation. In their eyes, I saw the flicker of recognition, the silent acknowledgment that something had shifted—that this monument was not just a tribute to the past. Among the faces in the crowd were Jason and Olivia, they seemed proud. On the other side was Mom, she had her phone out recording me. Claire was, of course, right in the front row, wearing a big smile. Her alone is enough to make me want to do this.

As the crowd fell silent, I took a breath and stepped forward, feeling a newfound sense of purpose rise within me. It was time to face the world, to accept the responsibility of what I had built. Thousands of citizens, all blending together, gathered before the towering structure I had spent the past year constructing.

The governor took the microphone before me, as planned, delivering a carefully crafted speech, praising the Monument as a testament to collective will. He spoke of progress, unity, and the need for stability in an increasingly unstable world. His words, designed to placate, to control, reinforced the illusion of harmony. I glanced at the Monument.

Inside the Monument lay a labyrinth of corridors and soaring chambers, each space a testament to the power of imagination. At the heart of the Monument stood the central chamber, bathed in the warm glow of reflected sunsets, the same type that was in Dad's library. A fractal-like shadow casts on the floor, taking after my beloved ficus tree's leaves. My own symbol of growth.

The Monument was a place for reflection and growth, too— where visitors could pause to contemplate the journey of humanity, its triumphs, tragedies, and the memories that had shaped us.

I stood at the podium with the governor, weariness and a trace of triumph marking my face. My eyes, usually flickering with restless energy, were fixed on the crowd. The camera lens focused on me felt cold, its calculated gaze stripping away any facade. It felt as though it could see straight through to the storm of doubts and anxieties that had plagued me for months. I shook off my nerves. The governor motioned for me to step up to the microphone.

"I stand here today, not just as the architect of this Monument, but as a reflection of all of us. Every one of us, working, striving, and pushing against limits we thought were unmovable. This Monument is not just stone and steel, it is the product of our collective will, our desire to overcome, to create, to leave something lasting.

This project, this dream, started with a single idea: a question of what it means to memorialize our existence. How do we capture our past and future in something that transcends time? What kind of legacy do we leave when the world around us is changing faster than we can comprehend?

We've faced our challenges. Doubts, criticism, setbacks. There were moments when I wondered if this Monument would ever be anything more than a vision I carried alone. But this isn't just my Monument—it's ours. It's all of you who contributed, who believed, who stood by me when I couldn't see the way forward. And for that, I am grateful.

What we've built here is more than just an object. It's a story, one that speaks to the complexity of who we are as a society, and as individuals. It's chaos within symmetry. It's the beauty of contradiction. A structure that rises and falls, that changes depending on your angle, depending on where you stand. A reflection of how we view the world—how we view ourselves.

It's not perfect. Perfection doesn't exist. Not in the world, and not in us. We're constantly evolving, constantly shifting. This Monument is no different. It's an exploration of our imperfection. Of the beauty found in our mistakes. It's about growth, and the understanding that our greatest triumphs come not from achieving perfection, but from learning, from struggling, and from continuing despite it all.

I want you all to look at this Monument and see yourselves

in it. See the history we've all shaped, the paths we've walked, the challenges we've overcome. It's a mirror of us—the good, the bad, the ugly. And yet, we stand here, in front of it, unified by our common experience.

This Monument represents not just what we've *done*, but what we're capable of. It's a symbol of our future. A future we have the power to shape. So let this Monument stand as a reminder of who we are, who we were, and who we have yet to become.

And as we look at this, let's not forget: we're still writing our story."

A moment of silence followed my last words, it seemed like forever, until slowly the crowd grew into a thunderous roar of clapping and cheering. The governor gestured for me to unveil the Monument. I hesitated for a brief moment, I took a deep breath and gave the signal to one of the engineers in the control room. The panels shifted and the steel walls parted. Or at least they tried to.

The walls to the Monument groaned as they slid. The mechanism whined, jolted, then stopped abruptly, leaving the doors to the interior corridors partially ajar. For a moment, silence hung over the crowd. My breath caught in my chest. I looked at the engineers in the back, their faces pale. I could feel the eyes of the crowd on me, waiting, judging. My fingers twitched at my side, torn between rushing to fix the problem or leaving it unresolved and running away to Claire. Maybe this was a sign. Maybe some things were better left unseen. The weight of perfection clawed at me again, that familiar voice whispering. But then, Claire's voice cut through the doubt in my mind, I thought of the times when I had to hide my sketches from being seen, I felt Dad's hand on my shoulder, and I heard Mom saying how she was so proud of me.

I exhaled, the tension in my shoulders easing as I stepped forward and placed my hands on the edge of the door. With a hard push, the mechanism jolted back to life, and the doors creaked open, revealing the Monument in full. Basking in the sun, light poured through the panels, creating a dazzling play of refractions and shadows. Then, as if by magic, the Monument came alive. Imperfect, but enough.

The faces of the crowd shifted from fear, to anticipation, to awe. They gasped, their eyes widening as they witnessed a glimpse of a world they had only heard whispers of. The Monument wasn't just a structure, it was a window into the soul of humanity.

A strange sense of liberation washed over me. The weight of expectation, the burden of the Monument, seemed to lift. I was free. I had spoken my truth.

The Monument stood before me, revealed in its full glory. The crowd's cheers were deafening, but I didn't hear them. All I could hear was the rush of my own heartbeat, the pounding in my chest as I looked at what I had created. What we had created. The fears, the doubts, the struggles—all of it seemed to dissipate in that one moment, replaced by something much more profound. Something I hadn't expected to feel.

As the noise from the crowd continued to swell, I turned to see Claire standing there, her smile wider than I'd ever seen. Her eyes shone with pride.

Every triumph, every failure, every lesson learned. And now, it was for everyone to see.

The crowd was still cheering, the applause vibrating through the air. I gave one last look to Claire, a silent acknowledgment that she had been with me through it all. With a final deep breath, I stepped back and stood at the finished canvas that stood before me.

Epilogue

The ripples from the Monument began to show subtly. Whispers in the workplace. Conversations in dim corners of sterile plazas. People began to reflect on the past, to talk about the world they had lost and the world they had created in its place. It wasn't a call to arms, but rather a gentle reminder. The Monument gave people a space to remember what once was, in the face of a world that constantly moved forward.

It stood as a silent witness to history, not a weapon, but a marker. A way to hold onto the essence of what we were. My father never fought against progress but sought to safeguard the essence of the past, and he would have understood that. He believed that the past should be woven into the fabric of our present and future.

In a way, the Monument was my attempt to carry forward his legacy. Not to change the course of history, but to remember it. Because in remembering, we protect the soul of humanity from being lost entirely in the rush to conform. Because I'm not one of the Gray Suits.

We didn't know what would come next, but *I* knew this was only the beginning. The Monument was the first step. I had a voice—and I would use it. The world was adapting, and I was going to be a part of it.

About the Author

Nathan is a full-time student and small business owner in Florida. When he isn't working or attending class he enjoys focusing on his passion for storytelling through photography and writing. His debut novella *The Last Monument* brings fresh perspectives to his writing, drawing inspiration from his experiences and the world around him. Nathan's background in political science coupled with his creative ability makes for a perfect story, exploring themes of societal control and philosophical expression.

You can connect with me on:

🌐 http://www.nates.pics

www.ingramcontent.com/pod-product-compliance
Lightning Source LLC
Chambersburg PA
CBHW060331310726
48976CB00007B/2520

9 798889 686390